THEIR VISCOUNTESS

THEIRS BOOK 5

JESS MICHAELS

For Michael.
He knows what he did.

PROLOGUE

Wren

Gilbert Wren stood in a parlor that was so familiar that it had sometimes felt like home. Sometimes it had felt like hell. He looked in every corner and there was a lifetime of memories to greet him. There was the doorway where he'd first met his two best friends a decade ago, and the fireplace where they'd first whispered secrets together as they had become closer over the years. He'd been sitting on that very settee at fifteen when he first felt…well, a great many feelings that had changed things…changed even more when he realized the two of them felt the same.

And yet because of their disparate positions, they had never been free to explore more together. So there had always been longing and nowhere to put the love they all felt. It had become grief over the years and the pain of it stung Wren's chest the way it always had.

It was almost fitting that they would have this meeting here. That the end would come exactly where the beginning had.

The door behind him opened and he turned to watch as Miss Emilia Harris and Aiden Edwards entered the room together. His two best mates, his two deepest loves, his dreams that could never come true. They were both so utterly beautiful. Emilia was tall and curvaceous with sleek, dark brown hair that was almost black in some lights and the bluest eyes Wren had ever seen on any person. She was the kind of woman people couldn't help but look at, the kind of woman artists sketched and poets waxed romantic about. His late father had been the man of affairs for *her* father, Mr. Harris, the second son of a baron.

And then there was Aiden. He was shorter than Wren, with broad shoulders and thick thighs. In centuries prior, he would have led warriors onto the battlefield with a broad sword lifted high. But alongside his thick strength, Aiden had an intelligent face, intense brown eyes and a smile that could light up the world. Like Wren, he'd been raised in service to Emilia's family, as his father was their longtime butler.

But he wasn't smiling now. None of them were as Emilia pressed the door closed behind them and leaned back on it with a sigh. "My father will be back soon," she said, her voice wavering a little as she dropped her gaze away from the men. "We'll have to hurry."

"You should have told me sooner," Wren said, hearing his own voice crack as he moved toward the pair of them. His pain was too intense, so he allowed anger to lead because it felt easier. "Both of you."

Aiden folded his arms and his waistcoat flexed against his broad chest in a distracting manner even in this moment. He arched a brow at Wren. "And just what would you have done?"

He ground his teeth. "Oh, yes, because you could do so much more, Aiden. And yet she spoke to *you* about it!"

He hadn't realized he was jealous of the confession Emilia had made until the words spilled from his lips. She pushed away from the door and stepped toward him, her gaze locked with his in sudden understanding. She moved between them, looking first at Aiden and then at Wren. She lifted a hand and pressed it gently against his chest. He could feel the weight of each finger even through the layers of fabric that separated them. His heart began to pound.

"Please," she said softly. "There's so little time. I know you're angry that we left you out."

"Why did you?" he asked, the air coming out of him with her touch. "We were always all of us or none of us. What changed?"

Aiden stepped closer. Now there was a thickness to the tension in the air. "Because you have a future that you could lose, Wren," he whispered. "You'll be a fine investigator one day, but I know that Mr. Boyd's apprenticeship isn't easy."

Wren pursed his lips. "No. He is exacting, that is for certain."

"And with Emilia's father paying for your apprenticeship, there is even more danger," Aiden continued. "Your chance could be taken if he found out you were interfering in what he wants for her. We couldn't risk it."

Wren tightened his jaw. In his heart he had known that was the reason. They had always tried to protect each other. Him especially, it felt like sometimes. And here they were.

He sighed. "I-I know. I just…wish I could save you, Emilia."

She shook her head. "In the end, neither of you can save me. We've tried every way, I promise you." She stepped away now, leaving a gap between him and Aiden that neither of them stepped to fill, even though what Wren wanted more than anything was to feel the support of Aiden's steady presence.

Emilia's eyes sparkled with tears before she turned her gaze away and whispered, "I…I will be forced marry Viscount Wilburn. I-I must accept it. I must accept."

And there it was. The destruction of Wren's heart in just a few sentences. The crushing of his whole world like it was no more than a paper dream. The loss of a future that made no sense and yet he had longed for it since he was fifteen.

"No," he whispered, not to stop her but just because he couldn't keep the word in.

Now Aiden did move forward and took Wren's hand. His strong fingers closed around Wren's and he squeezed oh-so-gently.

"Are you sure?" Wren asked, even though he knew the answer.

She nodded. "Certain. The contracts were signed last night. The wedding will be in a few weeks' time. There is no stopping it now."

"God," Wren said, and Aiden gripped his hand even tighter.

Emilia stared at the two of them for what felt like a lifetime, and then she stepped forward, her full lower lip trembling slightly. "I-I wanted to see you both. To talk to you both one more time because I know that will never be allowed once I'm married. The viscount would see, I know he would. He would know what my heart is if you were near me. And he would never let that pass, I don't think."

She eased closer once more and leaned in. Wren and Aiden did the same and their foreheads touched in a circle, their breath mingling and their emotions understood even if they weren't said. Wren turned his face and his lips brushed Emilia's jawline.

She caught her breath, her mouth finding his in a searing kiss. Their tongues tangled, heated desire brought to a boil after so many years, so many thwarted moments. There had also been a few not-so-thwarted, a few brief kisses between Emilia and each of them. A few caresses, sometimes with both the men holding her hand before they pulled away in shyness. After all, three people couldn't be in love. Society declared it so. And so over the years none of it had ever gone so far as his heated body wanted, what his most wicked fantasies created in his bed.

She broke away, her breath short, and then she pivoted toward Aiden. As Wren watched, Aiden cupped her cheek and the two of them kissed just as passionately. His body ached as he felt their desire, felt their love for each other, felt the desperation of the parting. When Emilia turned away from Aiden, she caught his hand and drew him closer to Wren.

"Kiss him," she said, her voice cracking as she looked at Wren. "You've always wanted it. This was never about me. It was always about us. And if this is the end, I want to *know*, to feel what I've always known was there between us. What could have been."

Wren's heart was pounding. Oh yes, he had adored and wanted Aiden Edwards for just as long as he'd wanted Emilia, even though they'd never acted on that desire either. But thoughts of the other man kept him up at night as often as thoughts of her…of all of them together. And now, in the heat of this moment that was likely their last, he had no way to refuse.

He stepped forward and pushed his fingers through Aiden's short, crisp hair. Aiden let out a soft sound of pleasure that was immediately lost on Wren's lips as they kissed. He was drowning in a desire more powerful than anything he'd ever felt and yet there was a wall there, an end that was coming that tempered the beauty of this moment.

Aiden pulled away first and there was a sparkle of tears in his eyes. One that made Wren's chest hurt even more.

Emilia stepped back, smoothing her gown. "If we can't all be together, I-I hope you two—"

"No." It was Aiden who said it, though the same answer had been on Wren's lips.

He shook his head and added, "We said a long time ago if it's not all of us, it's none of us."

"Wren," Emilia breathed. "Aiden. That was a promise of children, made about sneaking out to fish together. It was not about…not about this. Not about—"

"If it cannot be all of us, it will be none of us," Aiden repeated firmly. "Yes, I want Wren. We've never been able to hide it, at least not from you. But if it cannot include you, then it won't be complete. It would be spoiled after a while, a joining of grief, nothing more."

"We couldn't be happy without you," Wren said as he locked eyes with Aiden and saw that he would truly lose everything today.

Emilia bent her head, her breath coming shallow. "I hate this."

"It's the way of your world, Em," Wren said. "I wish we could save you, but the two of us are from another world. The son of a man of affairs and the son of a butler? We don't have the power, we wouldn't have it even if we were older, even if things were different."

She wanted to argue, Wren could see it. Her sense of right, of fairness, meant she judged people by their characters rather than their position in life. It was one of the most remarkable things about her. It was entirely unfortunate that Emilia couldn't rule the world. And that no matter how she wanted to change it, she had no more power to do so than they did.

"I hate that it's true. I hate it," she whispered. "I've tried so hard to find a way to make it not true."

Aiden squeezed her hand. "It's not your fault. It's not any of our fault."

She drew in a short breath before she nodded sadly. She slipped her hand away and then stepped away. "I-I'm going to try to be happy if I can, but you both must know that my heart will always have a place for you. That will never change. It can't."

"For me either," Aiden said softly.

"Nor for me."

They were silent for a moment and then Wren moved toward the door. "We'll go so that your father won't find us here. It will be difficult enough for you without us making it harder."

He was shaking as she opened the door to let them out but wouldn't meet his eyes. Perhaps it was for the best, at that. This was painful enough. "Good—goodbye, Emilia."

She let out a soft sob and all he wanted to do was turn around, hold her, run with her. But he was twenty, with very small prospects, almost no money and no power at all. He could only hurt her by trying to do what was impossible.

So he left her, hearing Aiden say something similar to her behind him. Gentle words of goodbye, of regret. Wren tried not to let them settle in his chest, nor the sound of her crying when Aiden followed behind him. Their horses were on the drive, side by side. Wren could hardly breathe as he turned toward Aiden.

They were silent as they stared at each other for what felt like an eternity and then Aiden shook his head. "We'll see each other in Town."

Wren nodded. "I'll look for you. I'm not going to lie and say I won't."

Aiden's breath exhaled shakily. "But we won't...we won't go to each other."

"If it's not all of us, it's none of us," Wren whispered yet again. "Even if it breaks our hearts. Even if it kills my soul."

"Goodbye, Wren," Aiden said, and swung up on his horse.

He rode away and only then did Wren seat himself and whisper, "Goodbye, love. Both my loves. Goodbye."

CHAPTER 1

Seven Years Later
Wren

It wasn't that Wren had never ridden by the home where Emilia had once lived, where he and Aiden had fallen in love with her and with each other all those years ago. He did so regularly, trying to will himself not to look at the place, always failing. In the last year, he had done so more often, drawn back by something he had seen on an investigation he'd taken. One he'd technically failed, though the man who hired him didn't know that. But it had reminded him of the love he'd been trying to stifle for so long.

Now, though, he passed by the tidy row home on his way to a far grander place. An estate he also sometimes visited, though he hated to pass by because he feared what he would see within its walls. He had been called there and he reached into the inside pocket of his great coat as his horse slowed in heavier traffic, and fingered the heavy sheet of paper with the address and the single line:

Your presence is requested by Viscount Wilburn.

Emilia's husband. Wren's stomach turned at the thought, but he still managed to guide himself the rest of the way to his destination. He was met by finely liveried servants and led into a beautiful parlor just off the foyer where tea awaited on an impeccably carved sideboard.

Everything about this place was elegant. He could see Emilia in it. Feel her presence in every corner and his heart ached.

The door behind him opened and he turned to watch Lord Wilburn enter the chamber. The man was older than Emilia by twenty years, which would put him in his mid-forties. He was very tall, though not quite as tall as Wren, and had an intensity to his gaze as he swept it over Wren.

"My lord," Wren said, and couldn't help but glance behind the man to see if Emilia would join them as well. He had to believe she was the reason behind him being called here. Yes, he had a reputation as an investigator for men of the viscount's ilk, but he couldn't believe that his arrival was a mere coincidence of his status.

"Mr. Wren, at last we meet," Wilburn said, his tone cold as the deepest winter. "Thank you for coming today."

Wren tried to behave as though this were a normal day, a normal potential client even, though his heart was racing out of control. "I will say I was confused as to why you summoned me. There were no details in your missive, which is out of the ordinary."

Wilburn motioned to the chairs before his fire and they sat, Wren trying not to worry his hands in his lap because he could feel his every move and word being judged.

"I thought that if I told you the reason for my request, you would not come," Wilburn said, and his tone somehow became icier. "Or that you would arrive with sword drawn rather than as you are now."

Wren wrinkled his brow. "I-I don't know what you mean."

"You keep glancing at the door," Wilburn said with the hint of a smile that held no friendliness. "You think you are being subtle about it, but it's obvious to me. You are looking for Lady Wilburn."

For what felt like a lifetime, Wren froze. The two men stared at each other as the clock ticked in the background. Wren clenched a hand around the armrest of his chair and at last he said, "Your wife, the viscountess. I assume you must know we were acquainted with each other as children, so I suppose I *did* believe she was the reason you called for me."

"Knew each other as children. Yes, that is one way to put it," Wilburn said softly. "Another way is that your father had dealings with hers. That you were allowed, by some miracle of her late father's ridiculous lack of boundaries, to be her *friend*. You and that other one...Mr. Edwards, the solicitor."

Wren felt his nostrils flaring. "You do know quite a bit. Yes, the three of us were friendly as children. Her father was a second son, but more interested in his obsessions and hobbies than in societal expectations."

"I ended that, though, didn't I?"

There was such a cruel bent to this man's words and to his growing smile. He seemed to be daring Wren to lash out and it took everything in him from doing just that.

"You and her father made an arrangement," he said as mildly as he could. "As so many of your rank do. It allowed him to continue with his work and you received a bride."

"A bride," Wilburn repeated. "But hardly a wife."

Wren flinched. "You obviously want to say something to me—why don't you say it and have it out? I don't have time for this game you seem to wish to play, my lord. I have other appointments today."

"I think you'll want to cancel those once you've heard my news," Wilburn said. "You see, you could look all day at the door for *Emilia*, but she'll never come. The viscountess was kidnapped yesterday morning."

Wren jumped to his feet at that abruptly given news as the cold hand of abject terror gripped his heart and squeezed. "What? Emilia kidnapped? What do you know? Have there been demands? Was she injured? Did you employ the guard to your cause?"

Wilburn didn't move from his seat and instead arched a brow. "Sit down, Mr. Wren."

Wren stared down at him, so cool and settled, with his hands folded on his knee as if they were discussing nothing more important than the weather. "How are you not panicked, Wilburn?"

"Because she was taken by your old friend, Aiden Edwards."

Wren sat back down with a thunk as he stared at Wilburn. "What?"

"Yes. Apparently his obsession with my wife, unlike your own, never cooled. He took her from this home yesterday—he was seen doing so by her maid. And given your past and the fact that his behavior must anger you...after all, you were once rivals for her, yes? Well, I thought *you* would be the perfect investigator to send to find them. To bring my wife back and make sure that the bastard who stole her will pay."

Emilia

Emilia sat on the bed in the master chamber in the cottage a day and a half's ride outside of London. She sighed, the sound ragged even to her own ears. The last two nights had been rough. Running from London, spending one night in a barn, another in the carriage Aiden had procured for them. Her neck hurt and her body felt heavy and restless.

What was she doing?

There was a light knock on the chamber door and she faced it as Aiden stepped inside. Her breath caught as she looked at him. For seven years she hadn't seen this man, seven years she had only dreamed of him and of Wren, until Aiden had reappeared briefly in her life, then at her window to sweep her away. He had changed and yet he was the same. Older now, his thick, muscular body was more fully formed and his cheeks were dark with a short, well-kept beard. He held himself with more certainty, with more sensuality.

And the tension that had existed between them when they were younger was even stronger now that she knew more about pleasure and desire and unfulfilled dreams.

"Is the room acceptable?" he asked.

She nodded. "It's very fine, Aiden."

"I checked the property and made some inquiries. It doesn't seem we've been followed," he said. "For now, at least, we'll be safe here. No one knows about this place."

"It's yours?" she asked.

"Yes. I was left it by a client two years ago as payment for a contract that delivered him a hefty sum. It was a secret little hideout for the gentleman and so it isn't well known."

Some of the fear that had been brewing in her chest eased. "Good. Good. Then we can breathe for a while. We can try to figure out what to do next. Or...or I can."

Aiden took a long step toward her. "You aren't alone, Emilia. I'm here."

She let her eyes flutter shut on a shaky sigh and tried to calm her pounding heart. She'd been alone for so long, isolated from the two people she loved most...and then isolated from even more than that as the marriage she had been forced into had disintegrated further and further. Become dangerous.

She'd been cornered into her most recent decisions by desperation and terror. But with Aiden standing across the room, she felt safe for the first time in years.

"Emilia."

He had moved while she sat with her eyes closed, his voice closer now. She opened them and looked up to find he was just in front of her. He caught her hand and drew her to her feet, intensity in the brown of his stare. By God, but she had missed him.

"Aiden," she whispered, just above a breath.

And then his mouth covered hers and breath departed her lungs entirely. His lips were firm and warm, but still gentle, just as he was gentle even though he was so much bigger than she was and could have forced her to do anything he wished. When was the last time she had encountered gentleness?

She couldn't remember and so she wound her arms around his neck and drowned in it now. Drowned in the way they opened their mouths at the same time and the kiss deepened. Their tongues warred and the gentleness of the caress became edged with need and desire and longing that had separated them for so long. She gripped the lapels of his jacket, lifting into him, trying to mold herself even closer as he tugged her to his chest and she felt the long, hard length of his strong body.

His hands glided down her back and his fingers smoothed along her backside, clenching slightly, pulling her against his erection.

She moaned and whimpered, "Oh my God."

Her voice seemed to pull him from his state and he drew back, staring down at her, searching her face for what felt like an eternity. Then he sighed. "We should send word to Wren."

Just his name made her heart throb even harder, but she shook her head. "I've done enough to hurt you—I can't hurt him too."

"But he'd want to know, Emilia," Aiden said as he released her and stepped back. "He could even help. He has connections through his vocation that I don't. We left him out last time, I don't want to regret doing it again."

She thought briefly of her husband. The viscount was not the kind of man who would let something be stolen from him. And *she* was his property, he had made that clear for a very long time. The law, she knew, would agree, and she feared what would happen then, and not just to her.

"I don't know," she whispered. "I'm afraid—"

Before she could finish that sentence, there was a loud pounding at the door to the cottage. They both froze and she stared at Aiden, seeing fear flash through his gaze.

"Hide," he said as he backed from the bedroom. "No one should know we're here."

Her hands were shaking as she hurried toward the long curtains that covered the window. She ducked behind them, careful that her slippers didn't stick out below the edge, and held her breath as she heard Aiden moving in the other room while the pounding at the door continued.

There was so much emotion to the racket, so much purpose. It had to be her husband. Somehow he must have found them and now everything would be lost and Aiden would be destroyed alongside her.

Tears filled her eyes and she blinked at them. She needed to be strong now, especially if she was going to find some way to save Aiden. Save herself. At least for a while.

"Who is it?" Aiden called out.

"It's me."

Emilia shoved the curtains aside at the sound of that voice outside. Even muffled through two doors, she knew it. Would have known it anywhere. Her heart soared with it, roared with it.

Wren. Wren was here, even though they hadn't called him. And she was afraid and thrilled in equal measure.

CHAPTER 2

Aiden

Aiden's hands shook as he turned the key in the lock and opened the door. He only had a moment to take in the tall, broad-shouldered man who was standing outside with the sunshine haloing him like some kind of angel before Wren shoved past him and into the cottage.

"What were you thinking?" he snapped with no preamble, despite the years that had separated them. He pivoted back at Aiden, face alive with emotion.

Aiden gulped in air as he shut and locked the door again. By God, but Wren was the same. Only…bigger somehow. His gorgeous face was rougher with stubble, though the full lips Aiden had dreamed about for so long were the same. His dark blue eyes were bright with anger, and yet as they moved over Aiden they were also filled with the same desire they always had been.

"Why are you here?" Aiden gasped out.

Wren folded his arms and shook his head. "I'm here because I was invited to Lord Wilburn's home yesterday afternoon. And he hired me to find you because he believes you kidnapped his wife. Please tell me you didn't kidnap his wife!"

The door to the bedchamber behind them clicked open at that shouted demand and both men turned. Emilia stepped out, her hands clenched at her heart, and Aiden felt the air come out of Wren just as it had come out of him the moment he saw her again after all those years of longing and loss.

"Wren," she whispered.

Wren was silent for a moment, just staring at her, and then he pivoted back on Aiden. "What the hell did you think you were doing, Aiden?"

"Will you report this back to him?" Aiden asked and immediately wished he could take the question back when Wren's expression fell, darkened.

"How dare you?" he whispered, his voice cracking. "How dare you ask me that."

Emilia lunged forward and wedged herself between them, keeping the tension from escalating with her presence. "Please!" she gasped out. Then she looked up at Wren. "How did you find us? Did he know where we were?"

Wren glared at Aiden. "No. I am an investigator. It's my job to find out things. And I would *never* tell that bastard a thing about either of you, not if he gave me a thousand pounds, a hundred thousand, a million."

"I'm sorry," Aiden said softly.

Wren bent his head and for a long, charged moment none of them said anything. Then he turned back to Emilia and caught her hands, drawing her in for a long hug. She clung to him, trembling, just as she had trembled when Aiden had done the same in his carriage after he swept her away. And he was so relieved to have Wren here, for them to all be together again.

He needed help. *She* needed help. They had always done better as a team.

"Come, let us talk," Wren said as he released her. "You two can explain yourselves and then we can work out what to do."

Emilia's gaze flitted to Aiden and he nodded slightly, encouraging her. She sighed and then moved to the settee in front of the roaring fire Aiden had set not half an hour before. He took the place beside her and Wren just stared at them. Then Wren drew in a shaky breath and, to Aiden's surprise, settled into the space on her opposite side. Emilia's breath hitched ever so slightly but none of them acknowledged the intimacy of the seating arrangement.

She looked toward Aiden and he reached out, covering her hand. "Tell him, just as you told me. He'll understand."

"I want to understand," Wren said softly, and reached across to stroke his own fingers across Aiden's. He shivered in response and so did Emilia. "Please."

They all pulled away and Emilia nodded. "I-I'll try," she whispered. "I'll try to tell you, but please understand this is difficult. So difficult."

Aiden ached for her as she drew long breaths over and over again, struggling for words. Wren said nothing as she did so, he simply held the space for her to find her own way. And at last, she did.

"I tried to be happy in my marriage," she said softly. "I knew I couldn't have what I wanted and I *tried* to be settled with what I had. I had nothing in common with Wilburn, but he was not unkind…at least at first."

"Emilia," Wren breathed, his expression crumpling ever so slightly.

She shrugged, tears brightening her expression. "The changes happened so slowly over the years. He became more distant, and then more sharp and then cruel in his words."

"Why?" Wren breathed.

"Because he wanted heirs and spares and I didn't provide them," she explained, her cheeks staining red. "God, how he hated me for it. *Despised* me for it. In the last few years, especially, he would rail at me about what a bad trade he made in me as a wife. And in the last year—"

She broke off and turned her head. Aiden squeezed her hand gently and she looked at him, her eyes bright with tears. Clearly she couldn't continue and so he drew a shaky breath and said, "Emilia believes that he…that he tried to kill her."

~

Emilia

Emilia felt like she was going to vomit as Aiden said the words she, herself, couldn't. That feeling multiplied as Wren sank back against the settee cushions, his expression shocked and pale. She was dragging the two people she loved more than any other into something so ugly and cruel. It was what she'd tried to prevent for years as she lived her lonely life and only dreamed of them.

"Wh-why do you think that?" Wren stammered at last, his voice trembling now.

She swallowed hard. "I got very ill a few months ago. I thought little of it until our cook whispered to me not to eat the soup. She was terrified and I didn't understand. I didn't want to, I suppose. But I realized that night that Wilburn *never* ate it. I-I believe he was poisoning it. When I stopped eating it, I got better. And his frustration with me multiplied as I recovered. He then became very vocal that his life would be better if I were dead."

Wren pushed to his feet and started for the door. "I'll kill him myself. I'll kill him with my bare hands."

Aiden was up before Emilia could be. He caught Wren's arms, yanking him back, keeping him from exiting the cottage. Wren fought him for a moment and then turned, collapsing against him as he shook.

"I know," Aiden whispered close to his ear. "I know, I felt the same way when Emilia reached out."

"Then how can you not want to rip him apart?" Wren growled.

"If you think I don't then you have forgotten a great deal about me," Aiden said. "But my main goal is to *protect* Emilia. And storming off to confront her husband may not do that. It *could* make things worse."

Wren's jaw tightened and Emilia caught her breath. She knew that look so well—Wren had always done that when he was frustrated. Then he let out a ragged sigh and rested his head forward on Aiden's shoulder. She was warmed by their support of each other.

"What can we do?" Aiden asked softly.

Wren lifted his head and stepped back, running a hand through his thick, dark hair and making himself look attractively bed-tousled in the process. He paced for a moment, his lips thin.

"I can...I can write some letters to the man about my so-called investigation," he said, nodding as if in agreement with his burgeoning plan. "I'll use contacts so that they seem to come from far away. I'll draw him off the track with false leads. And it will buy us some time to decide how to best proceed."

"Thank you," Emilia said, relief flooding her, not just that he had ideas in mind that might help her, but also that he was no longer intent on rushing off to confront her husband.

Wren glanced toward Emilia, holding her gaze steady. "What you've been through, I...I cannot imagine. Though I always knew your strength, I see it even more here now."

Emilia's breath caught. "I fear I haven't earned that compliment, Wren. I haven't felt strong in the last seven years. All I've done in that time is try to survive. And missed you." She looked toward Aiden behind Wren. "Both of you. I missed...*us* all these years. What kept me going was dreaming of you two...thinking about what could have been."

Wren stared at her for a long moment and then he closed the distance between them in a long step. He reached his hand up to touch her cheek, traced the line of it until his fingers glided into her hair. She couldn't breathe now, just stare into the darkness of his blue eyes and feel all the passion and love and desire she had lacked in her years as Lady Wilburn.

And when he bent his head to kiss her, she surrendered to it, just as she had to Aiden before Wren's arrival. But where Aiden had been gentle, Wren was something different. Not cruel, never that, but more demanding, more forceful. She opened to him, lifting against his chest, losing herself in his warmth and protection.

"I'm sorry," he said, pulling away with a shake of his head.

"I'm not," she whispered. "I never could be."

Aiden stepped up, his pupils dilated with clear desire after seeing Wren kiss her. It made Emilia shiver to see it. To feel the crackling tension between them all.

"You must be exhausted, Wren," Aiden said. "Can I get you tea?"

Wren nodded. "Yes."

"Sit with her and I'll prepare it." He smiled at them both and then slipped away, allowing Emilia a moment alone with Wren.

He motioned to the settee where they sat together and he caught her hand in both of his, cradling and protecting her with just the barest touch. "I cannot believe I'm here with you," he said.

She smiled up at him, drinking him in. He really was beautiful, not changed at all in the years that had separated them and yet deeply changed. His dark blue eyes were the same, his full lips, the way he looked so deeply into her eyes when he spoke to her, like she was the only person in the whole world. But he had grown into himself, as well. He was more broad-shouldered and though it was evident he was usually clean-shaven, he had stubble slashed across his cheeks that only highlighted that his face had become more angled.

"You are beautiful," she whispered. "I had forgotten how beautiful."

"Hmmm," he said, and pushed a lock of her hair away from her face. "I think that's my line."

She laughed a little, the sound rusty after so long of no use. "You must have been shocked when Wilburn called you to him."

"I thought it was your doing," he said, and his gaze grew distant for a moment. "I could hardly breathe with the idea that I would see you, stand with you after all this time. And then I stopped breathing entirely when he told me what he thinks he knows and I realized you were in danger."

She nodded. "I'm so sorry you had to go through that."

"Again," he whispered. "That's my line."

They were quiet for a moment, just looking at each other. And then Emilia dared to draw in another deep breath. "I used to dream of you. Of both of you."

He shifted and his pupils dilated with desire. "Did you now? And what did you dream."

She stood on shaky legs and drew him up with her. "That you would kiss me like you did a moment ago."

"But this isn't a dream," he whispered, and then his mouth came back to hers as she wound her arms around his neck and leaned into his solidness and warmth once again.

She lost herself in that for a moment, savoring the feel of this man with his arms around her. It was only when Aiden returned to the room that she became aware of her surroundings again. There was the clatter of him setting the tea service down on a table, but she didn't break her mouth from Wren's. She couldn't. She needed him more than she needed breath in that moment. Needed so much more than just him.

And it was like Aiden understood that, for in that moment, she felt another set of hands on her back. She shivered as her lips parted from Wren's and she looked over her shoulder to find Aiden behind her. He stood very still for a moment, one hand on her hip, the other against her ribcage. Then he leaned in and his mouth found the side of her throat. She whimpered and lifted her lips back to Wren.

He groaned as he returned to kissing her and she gripped his lapels as sensation began to mob her. This was what she'd dreamed of, foggy dreams when she was younger, before she knew what the physical union between lovers was like. After her marriage, the dreams had become sharper, more powerful. And eventually they had been the only thing she could do to endure her husband's touch. She would close her eyes and pretend it was one of these men.

And when she was alone in her bed?

Well, she dreamed of them both, touching her as they were now, fingers gripping against the fine silk of her gown. She'd dreamed of them having her in so many ways as she arched against her own fingers in her lonely bed.

Wren drew back, his fingers smoothing against her jaw. "Should we do this?" he whispered. "You're married and you've been through so much."

She blinked up at him, hating how he was bringing reality to this fantasy. Hating that Aiden lifted his mouth away from her throat, as if Wren's words had brought him out of the spell between them, too.

"My marriage was over the moment I believed my husband could kill me," she said softly. "And I want this. I've always wanted this, wanted both of you. Whatever is going to happen next, I...I need this. I need both of you. Together. Now, while we still have the chance."

She turned a little and caught Aiden's chin, drawing him to her. She kissed him, darting her tongue out to taste him, feeling the growl from deep in his chest as it reverberated through her. Then she turned back and pulled Wren down to her the same way.

"Please, forget everything but this. Let me forget everything but this, too."

He stared into her eyes for a long moment and then he nodded, his mouth coming back to hers, his hands drawing up into her hair, pulling it down around his fingers as she arched against him, ground back against Aiden. Their bodies were so hard as she was wedged between them. Hard chests, hard cocks, one pressed to her belly, another against her backside. She shivered at the feel of them, at the promise of what was about to happen next.

She felt them moving as a unit, Wren guiding her back through the door to the bedroom where she had been hiding not an hour before. Aiden followed, his hands gliding over her hips, massaging her there.

"Look at me," Wren said as he drew back yet again.

Emilia's gaze felt blurry as she forced herself to do so, staring up into that gorgeous face. "Y-Yes?"

"If you want to stop, we stop," he said. "Either of you."

She nodded and glanced back over her shoulder at Aiden. He had a half-smile on his face as he leaned over her shoulder and bunched his fingers into Wren's cravat, tugging him closer.

"I'm not going to want to stop, Wren," he promised before he hauled Wren in for his own kiss.

Emilia could hardly breathe as their tongues tangled before her, their passion for each other as powerful as theirs for her. Oh yes, she would enjoy this ultimate fantasy. She would forget the truth that it couldn't last. And she would lose herself in everything she had ever wanted.

Wren turned her to face Aiden and she lifted up to wrap her arms around him, kissing him. He drove his tongue into her now, no longer gentle, but purposeful, hungry. She felt Wren's hands along the buttons at her spine and her breath caught as he unfastened the first one and dropped his lips to the tiny bit of skin he had revealed. He repeated the action on the next button, the next, until he reached the edge of her chemise and traced the line of lacy across the top with his tongue.

"You're so sweet, Emilia," he murmured against her skin. "I can't wait to taste you all over."

"Please," she murmured against Aiden's lips, and he chuckled without breaking their kiss.

Wren was pushing her gown forward. Aiden caught the bodice and helped. Hands slid down her body and with her eyes shut she began to lose herself, uncertain who was cupping her breast through her chemise and who was sliding thumbs into the folded fabric of her gown to guide it past her hips.

And it didn't matter who, really. They were one now, moving toward an ultimate pleasure that she had longed for. She pulled away from Aiden's mouth and forced herself to look at him. Aiden's pupils had dilated with desire and he played with the strap of her chemise, stroking it between his thumb and forefinger before he guided it down to her elbow.

"You don't know how many times I imagined this," he said, and lowered the other strap. "Seeing you like this. Touching you like this." The fabric fell away from her breasts and she was naked from the waist up.

Heat filled her cheeks at being so revealed. She had never liked showing herself to her husband, who only had criticisms for her body that had grown louder as she pleased him less and less. But when Aiden looked down at her, all she saw was his admiration, his adoration and she forced herself not to lift her hands and cover her breasts.

"Gorgeous," Aiden whispered as he bent his head and traced his tongue around her nipple. "Perfect."

She glided her fingers into his hair, holding him there as he licked and sucked and sent lightning bolts of pleasure through her body. As she began to moan, Wren ground against her backside, his hands bunching the fabric of her chemise at her hips.

"I love that sound," he whispered against her ear, sucking gently on the lobe.

She moaned again. She couldn't have stopped herself for all the gold in England, and Wren chuckled against her. Aiden looked up at him from his place at her breasts and smiled.

"I want to watch you," he whispered, his breath short. "I want to watch you have her before we share her."

CHAPTER 3

Emilia

As Emilia's head spun from Aiden's request, she heard Wren's breath catch at her back. He let out a garbled moan deep from his chest. "Do you want that, Emilia?"

She blinked at the question. To be watched by Aiden, to be taken by Wren? The possibility swept her off her feet, crashed dreams into reality, and all she could manage was a jerky nod of consent. Aiden kissed her again and then turned her to Wren. She looked over her shoulder at him as he backed toward the door to the bedchamber. He closed it and leaned back against it, rubbing the hard cock that flared his trousers slightly.

Wren touched her chin and brought her attention back to him. "I want to make you come, Emilia," he whispered. "I want to feel you come around my cock until you're weak."

"Please," she whimpered. "But I want to see you, Wren. I need to see you."

He nodded and stepped back, shoving out of his jacket and tossing it on the floor where her dress had been kicked. She watched him, licking her lips as he slowly untied his cravat, unbuttoned his shirt and tugged it over his head. She heard Aiden make a sound from the door and glanced back to find he had unbuttoned the fall front of his trousers and was now stoking his rigid, naked cock. She wished she could see him better, but the thought that he was doing it made her wild with excitement.

She forced her attention back to Wren. He was gorgeous. There was no other word for the body presented to her. Muscular, but still lean. His broad shoulders tapered down to narrow hips and in between was a length of hard muscle lightly peppered with dark chest hair.

Emilia couldn't help herself. She staggered a step forward and placed a trembling hand to the bare skin, bunching her fingers against the warm firmness of his form. He pushed his hand into her hair, tilting her face up to kiss her hard and fast. She shivered because Wren had always been the one in control and yet she felt him balancing on the edge of it now. Ready to unleash whatever passions he repressed for public consumption.

He gripped the edge of her chemise, which was still bunched at her hips, and tugged hard. It fluttered to her feet and now she was naked but for her stockings, her slippers. He stepped away and stared at her for a long, charged moment. Then he faced her toward Aiden to show him what he saw.

His body moved against her back and his arms came around her, drawing her against his bare chest. "Look at her," he whispered.

"I couldn't look away if I tried," Aiden said, his strokes on his cock harder now, faster.

Wren cupped her breasts, squeezing the sensitive flesh, lifting her as he rubbed his thumbs against her nipples. She ground back against him with a soft cry, trying to find some way to relieve the throbbing pleasure that had already begun to make her thighs wet with anticipation.

One of his hands stole away from her breast, sliding down her ribcage, her stomach, and then settled between her legs. She lolled her head against his chest, the air leaving her lungs when he rubbed thick fingers across the lips of her sex.

"She's so wet, Aiden," he said. "So ready for me, for you, for us."

Aiden nodded, his teeth sinking into his lower lip the same way Emilia wanted to sink her own into it. Wren's fingers slid across her entrance again and she spread her legs farther to allow him access. He stroked into her, finding no resistance, and she barked out pleasure at the invasion.

He thrust with his fingers, gently but insistently, playing her body like an instrument he had been practicing all his life. She rocked against him, her breath short as the pleasure built. He never took her too far, though, never let her find release, just teased her. Played with her as if they had all night.

And, of course, they did. That fact was as powerful as his touch after all these years apart. She reached back and rubbed her hand against the front of his trousers, feeling the hardness of him, the rumble of pleasure in his chest.

She turned in his arms to face him and smiled up at him. "I want to see all of you," she whispered.

He cupped her face and kissed her again, deeply and slowly. Then he motioned to the bed. She followed the silent order and climbed up, resting back against the pillows, spreading her legs a little so that Aiden could see her. He moved forward and she wanted so much for him to touch her, but instead he took a chair and turned it toward the bed.

"Look at me," Wren said softly.

Her attention shifted to him as ordered. He unfastened his fall front and shoved his trousers away. She caught her breath as she stared at him in all his naked glory. His cock was as beautiful as everything else about him: thick and long and so hard as it curled against him, a proud declaration of everything he wanted to do to her.

She glanced at Aiden and found he was just as fascinated. His eyes were a little glazed, his mouth slightly slack as he stared just as she did, at this man they had both adored for so long.

"You're going to get everything you want, Aiden," she said softly, and then smiled at Wren. "We're all going to get what we want."

He nodded as he came to the bed. He leaned in to kiss her again and then drew back to whisper, "I want to show him, Emilia. Let's let him see."

She nodded, unable to do anything else when he was so close, when what she'd dreamed of was so close. He tugged her into a seated position and she instantly moved onto her knees as he lay down, his head toward the bottom of the bed.

"Ride me," he grunted, his voice rough.

She shifted over him, rubbing her body along his as she put herself in position to straddle him. She glanced up and saw that Aiden had leaned forward in his chair, staring at them. She smiled at him as she lifted slightly and caught Wren's naked cock in her hand. He groaned as she stroked him once, twice, and then aligned him with her wet body. There was no resistance as she dropped down over him, taking him inside with one thick, heavy thrust.

She was being impossibly stretched and she arched her back, grinding against the fullness that was so delicious. When she looked down at Wren, he was staring at her, watching every reaction on her face. She began to rock over him, never breaking eye contact, savoring each pleasurable moment of this, memorizing the way he felt inside of her. The way his hands felt as they gripped her hips while she rode him.

And oh, how she rode him, grinding against him, gripping him with every thrust, her breath coming faster as pleasure mounted deep in her body. She had never before come so close to the edge of release so fast and yet here she was, her body starting to shake as pleasure notched up between her legs, becoming sharper and more focused.

"Fuck, Emilia," Wren groaned, the veins in his neck becoming more pronounced as he lifted to meet her thrusts and stimulated her sensitive body all the more.

When she fell, she shouted, her hips rolling out of control, her fingernails digging into his shoulders as wave after powerful wave of pleasure unlike anything she'd ever known raced through her. It seemed to go on forever, like a storm that had been unleashed and now raged until she was weak and flopped forward on his body. His arms came around her, his mouth hot and heavy on hers as she panted out the remnants of her release.

"God, that was gorgeous," Aiden panted as he got to his feet. "Emilia, your face when you come is art."

She blushed at the compliment, even as she sat back up, Wren's cock still hard inside of her, and reached for Aiden. He kissed her, resting his hand on Wren's chest as he did so. Wren surged up at the touch with a moan.

"I want to taste her," Aiden said, still looking at Emilia, but obviously talking to Wren.

Wren smiled, his pupils dilated until there was almost no blue left, and nodded. Emilia shifted, putting her head back on the pillows and spreading her legs for Aiden.

Only he didn't bury his head between them. Instead he pressed the hand on Wren's chest a little harder and put his mouth around Wren's cock, where he began to lick and suck.

Emilia moaned at that intimate sight of it, her fingers going to between her legs to the wetness there, the sensitive clitoris where she began to play as she watched the show before her.

Aiden

Aiden had dreamed of sucking Wren off for years. When he fucked men in clubs, it was always Wren's face he pictured, always Wren he dreamed of. And now he had his hard cock in his mouth and he swirled his tongue around the thick length of it. Better yet, he could taste the salty-sweet heaven of Emilia's powerful release with every lick.

"I want to come in her," Wren gasped, even as he held Aiden's head in place and fucked his throat lightly. "With you."

Aiden smiled around him and looked up without separating his mouth from him. He bobbed up and down a few more times, taking Wren to the edge, and then he popped his hard cock free.

"Do you want that, Emilia? Both of us inside of you?"

"Yes," she moaned, her voice shaky and needy. "I need you both now!"

Aiden dragged his hand down the length of Wren's body as he moved to Emilia. Her blue eyes were wide, her hand flicking across her sex restlessly. He caged her in on the pillows, living for the way her breath caught as he lowered his mouth and kissed her. She moaned, her arms coming around his shoulders, her hips lifting toward him.

"I want to take my time with you," he murmured against her mouth. "I want to make you beg for me, for him, for this. I want to take you to the edge over and over until you explode with such power that you nearly lose consciousness."

She shuddered with a mewl of needy pleasure at the image he created.

"But right now if I don't have you, if I don't feel you both, I think I might expire."

"Good," she gasped. "Because I can't wait."

He gripped her hips and slid her downward on the bed. "Wren," he said without looking at him. "In my bedside table you'll find what you'll need to make it easier for her."

Wren shifted, his weight coming off the bed. He dragged his nails along Aiden's back as he walked and Aiden arched a little at the abrasion of his sensitive skin. He had never felt so alive in his entire life. So filled with love and desire all at once. He never wanted it to end. He wanted to stay in this fantasy forever.

So he fully surrendered to it as he dropped his head between her legs and began to lick her. She gasped at the motion and lifted toward him, grinding against him as her moans turned to wails of pleasure. He'd tasted her on Wren's cock, but the full flavor of her release was even better. He sucked her clitoris, swirling his tongue around the hard nub, reveling in how her legs shook almost immediately. Wren had laid that path for him and now her responsive body followed it.

When she came, her fingers clenched his scalp, her body trembled and he had to hold her hips steady so she didn't flop them both off the high bed. He glanced up to find Wren standing beside them, slightly slack jawed as he stared, a bottle of oil in his hand.

Aiden smiled up at him as he moved to his back and motioned Emilia toward him. "Just like with Wren, I want you to ride me. And then he'll come behind you and take your arse."

Her eyes went wide and she looked at Wren. He swallowed hard. "Do you want that, Emilia?"

She nodded. "Yes. I want that so much."

"I'll make you ready," Wren promised as she shifted to her knees and crawled toward Aiden, straddling him as she licked a path along his stomach, up his chest and finally took his lips.

Their tongues tangled, at first gently and then harder as she positioned herself above him. He caught his breath as she maneuvered him to her entrance and then lowered herself onto him inch by inch. The grip of her, the wet heat, it was almost too much after so many years of waiting and longing and dreaming. Emilia was better than he'd ever imagined.

She rocked over him, her breath coming short, her body clinging to his as she threw her head back and let out a low, hungry moan. A moan that grew deeper as Wren positioned himself on his knees behind her. He kissed her shoulder as he watched Aiden, a small smile on his normally serious face.

He coated his fingers in oil as he stared and Aiden surged harder beneath Emilia as he watched Wren's fingers move between the globes of her bottom and begin to stroke her.

It was in that moment Aiden realized this was truly going to happen. And he had to fight not to be unmanned right then and there before they had even fully begun.

CHAPTER 4

Emilia

Emilia was overwhelmed by sensation at a level she had never experienced before. Aiden's hard cock in her, stimulating her already aching clitoris with every swirling thrust of their bodies, and now Wren, his firm, thick fingers working against her arse, opening her for what was yet to come. She was pleased there were no servants in the house, for she couldn't hold back her moans and cries of pleasure as she surrendered her body fully to these men. Her men.

"Ready, angel?" Wren whispered behind her as she felt the thick head of his cock at her backside.

"Yes," she moaned. "Oh, please, yes."

He gripped her hips as Aiden stopped moving momentarily. There was not a breath taken between them as Wren pressed against her, slowly taking her. Pain met with pleasure as he opened her unused channel. Then pleasure won the battle as he slowly seated himself within her. She felt so full with them, so achingly, perfectly full, as if it had always been meant to be this way.

"Can you feel each other?" she moaned.

Aiden jerked out a nod. "Yes," he gasped. "I can feel him. It's so good, Wren. You feel so good."

"You too," Wren murmured as he slid back and then forward again, causing both Emilia and Aiden to cry out.

She couldn't hold back anymore. She returned to rocking over Aiden as she held tight to his shoulders. Wren matched his strokes to her rhythm, his hands gripping her hips. She would have marks there later. She wanted them, his fingers tattooed on her skin forever.

Wren's mouth found her shoulder—he licked and nipped her flesh as she began to ride harder and faster. Pleasure so powerful she almost feared it was rising in her, coming from every part of her body. It flowed through her, making her limbs light and her body clench against it. The men were relentless, not giving her respite from the wild sensations until she bucked, nearly unseating both of them as she screamed through the powerful orgasm that roared through her.

Her gripping body had clearly driven them to the edge, too. Both of them increased their tempos, clenching tighter against her flesh. Wren released her with one hand and reached out, his fingers tangling with Aiden's. He moaned, the sound echoed by Wren, and then they were both coming, filling her until she went weak with it and collapsed on Aiden's chest.

She had no idea how long they lay together after, her sprawled over Aiden, their bodies still joined. Wren with his head against her hip, his fingers playing along Aiden's thick thigh. All she knew was that she never wanted to move from this place, she never wanted this to end.

But it had to.

She shifted at last and groaned as Aiden's cock slipped from her body. Wren moved so she could roll onto her back and stare up at the ceiling above in silence.

"That was everything I ever wanted," Wren said softly.

She glanced down at him. He was watching her, concern on his face. Aiden was too. Her two protectors. Except what could they do to keep her safe except wreck themselves? In some ways it was no different than it had been when they were younger. Oh, they both had more resources now, more power. But it wouldn't be enough when faced with her husband.

"Please don't look so forlorn," Aiden said, leaning up to kiss her. "Let us have the pleasure of what we just did for a while longer, at least. Now, Wren, why don't you and I go prepare a bath for our fair lady? Rest, Emilia. Rest at last and don't fret over the future."

She nodded and watched as they got up, dressed themselves, helping each other here and there, sharing smiles, their connection plain. She ached as she watched it, a lovely, happy ache that she hadn't felt in so long. And as they left her, she sighed and closed her eyes. Perhaps the future wasn't certain, but for now she was safe.

So she slept for the first time in weeks and knew that the two men who had just loved her so well would keep her from harm. She just hoped she could do the same for them.

Aiden

Even though Aiden and Wren had both spent their passions less than half an hour before, the tension between them was still thick as they walked together to the kitchen in the cottage. There was already a big pot there, bubbling with hot water.

"You were preparing," Wren said softly.

Aiden nodded. "I put it on when I made the tea we abandoned in the other room. I thought she'd need something to relax. She's been ragged from fear for weeks."

Wren shut his eyes and his expression tightened. Aiden caught his breath, for he knew that look well. Wren working to fix a problem. For the first time since he'd received Emilia's plea for help, he believed they might be able to save the day. Together.

"Come, there's a pump behind the cottage," Aiden said. "We'll get more water first and then take that pot up to the tub."

Wren followed him and they exited through the servants' entrance at the back of the kitchen. There were two buckets already at the pump and Aiden began working at it first to fill one. Wren watched a slight smile on his face.

"You look absolutely gorgeous doing that, you know," he said.

Aiden laughed, though the compliment made him very aware that his body was still throbbing with need despite the powerful experience earlier.

"I'm sure you will, as well." He wiped his brow and then continued at the pump. "So why did Emilia's husband call on you to find us?"

Wren stiffened. "Still worried about my motives?"

Aiden stopped pumping and stepped around to him. He caught Wren's arms and pulled him in for a kiss. He'd meant it as a quick moment of comfort, but Wren had other ideas. He dragged Aiden closer, their bodies molding together as the kiss deepened, their tongues warring and then slowing until it was a gentle, erotic exploration of each other.

When they parted, they were both panting with the power of it. Aiden managed to gather himself and step back. "I'm sorry about what I asked earlier," he said. "We were running for two days. Your arrival was so unexpected, but I know you, Wren. No matter how long we've been apart, I know you would *never* be party to harming either Emilia or me."

Wren's expression softened slightly and he nodded. "Good. I can't imagine how difficult this has been for you. For her."

"For her it's been so much worse," Aiden whispered. "Her nightmares…"

He trailed off and bent his head. Wren reached out and touched his hand. "You saved her. As for me…" He sighed. "Well, I believe the viscount believes he can manipulate me. He knows we have a past, the three of us. But he thinks you and I were rivals for her."

Aiden had bent his head to return to the water but now he wrenched his gaze up to Wren. For a moment they stared at each other and then Wren started to laugh. Aiden couldn't help but join in at the ridiculousness of that belief.

"Oh yes, rivals," Aiden said when he could finally breathe past his humor. "That's exactly what it felt like less than an hour ago."

"An intense rivalry to be certain," Wren said, though his tone was becoming more seductive. "Who will break first and lose control?"

"We should wager on it next time."

Wren's expression went darker with desire. "As long as Emilia wins the race, I'm happy to try to break you after."

"A bargain," Aiden said, and extended his hand. Wren's fingers stroked over his and then he released him.

"Since I don't think it would be appropriate to do all the things I'd like to do to you out here, why don't you let me fill the second bucket with water so we can go inside and get back to the very fair lady in our bed?"

Aiden moved the full bucket of water and stepped aside so Wren could work on the second one. He watched him move for a while, appreciating his form as much as his own had been appreciated a few moments before.

"I have my own questions, you know," Wren said and glanced up at him.

"And what are those?"

There was a hesitation and Aiden tensed slightly, this time not with pleasure. It seemed they were very serious questions, indeed.

Wren cleared his throat. "Why *did* she come to you?"

And there it was, the remnants of a pain that had existed for a long time. He and Emilia had always tried to protect Wren. He had more to lose, after all. Further to fall. And Wren had always hated it, being pushed outside of the pain so he wouldn't be ruined.

"You know I became a solicitor after we lost each other."

"Yes," Wren said softly, but Aiden heard the intense pride in his voice. The same he felt when he saw how Wren had raised himself up.

He smiled. "Emilia had insisted her father pay for the apprenticeship, just a he paid for yours, as a reward for my father's years of service as his butler. I went to the side of the old man's own solicitor and took over his practice when he died a few years ago."

"You took over her father's estate work," Wren breathed.

Aiden nodded. "Yes. When her father died, I was responsible for the distribution and settling of his small estate," Aiden explained. "I saw her once last year after the death. It was only in passing, but she was... God, she looked so small with the pain she was trying to hide. I wanted to touch her so badly, to hold her, but Wilburn was always lurking. Now I realize that must have been part of her abuse, not to let her see a friend, someone he believed once had feelings for her."

"Once," Wren whispered.

"I doubt he believed that those kinds of emotions could last after so many years parted. He was too small minded and cruel to be able to picture that one could love without hope for decades, a lifetime, as we had all planned to do when we were so ruthlessly parted."

Wren trembled and his hand faltered on the pump handle. "So because she saw you..."

"She knew my address from the estate paperwork that required her signature. Her father had left her a little pin money separate from Wilburn. Perhaps at the end he knew the mistake he'd made in matching her. I don't know. But in her desperation she reached out to me."

Wren's bucket was full and he straightened from the pump. His blue eyes were midnight with emotion and glimmered with unshed tears. "What did she say?"

"Just two lines," Aiden choked out. "I will see them dance before my eyes until the day I die. *I need you, Aiden. Please help me.*" He drew in a few breaths to calm himself at the memory. "She didn't even sign it. I suppose she feared it might be intercepted and then she could claim ignorance. But I knew it was her. I knew her hand-writing."

"So you swept in and kidnapped her," Wren said.

"Is it kidnapping if the abductee wishes to run with you, to never look back?" Aiden asked.

"No. You saved her," Wren corrected. "Thank God you saved her."

"It was only when we were out of London that she stopped shaking. That she felt safe enough to tell me the same story she told you. And she wept. And screamed. And clung to me. Clung to me all night as we slept in a barn because she feared being found out if we took a room at an inn on the route."

"And had nightmares," Wren said.

Aiden nodded. "Yes." He watched Wren carefully now. He was unreadable. Aiden supposed he sometimes had to be that in his profession. "I promise you, love, we weren't trying to lock you out."

"And yet you did. You could have called for me the moment you received her note. You could have included me." There was an edge to his voice as he said those words.

Aiden took his hand. "We were trying to protect you."

"I don't need protection, Aiden." Wren tugged his hand away and ran it through his hair with a ragged breath of frustration. "*She* does. And without both of us involved, we won't be able to provide it."

"We're both involved now," Aiden whispered. "And we'll make certain she is safe."

Wren nodded and then glanced up at the house. "And what about all the other things we could make certain she was?"

Aiden shifted. "You're talking about what we just did. You're talking about our bond with each other."

"Yes."

For a long moment, Aiden didn't answer as he relived all those powerful moments in that bed in the cottage. "If she wants to continue, I see no reason why we should deny ourselves. She deserves all the pleasure in the world after what she's endured."

"Good." Wren picked up his full bucket of water and then leaned in to gently kiss Aiden. "Then we're agreed. Now why don't we go up and continue?"

Aiden watched Wren go into the house, enjoying the view of his toned shoulders as they strained against the weight of the full bucket. But his pleasure was tinged with worry. Here they were in a fantasy land, and he would revel in it as long as it lasted. But the real world still existed and its real threats. None of them could forget that if they wanted to get out of this alive.

CHAPTER 5

Emilia

Emilia was having the most wonderful dream. She was in a big bed with warm, soft bedding and she was being touched. Gently and with only her pleasure as a goal. And it wasn't just anyone touching her, but it was Wren and Aiden, their big hands crossing and interlocking as they made her arch. She felt so safe, so happy that she knew it must be a dream.

Only as they continued to stroke her skin, something changed. She felt a tension enter the room. Their smiles began to shift to frowns and then fear. Fear that pierced her, as well. She wanted to sit up on the bed and look for the threat that had entered this safe realm, but she was suddenly trapped, held down, helpless to do anything but watch as Wren and Aiden both gasped and then dissolved into smoke.

And out of that smoke walked Wilburn. Her husband smiled as he reached for her.

"My faithless whore of a wife," he said, his eyes bright with rage and cruelty and a promise of pain and death.

She did sit up then, shoving at the bedclothes, kicking at nothingness as she shrieked. The door to the small adjoining dressing room flew open and Aiden rushed through. He caught her in his arms, pulling her flush against his naked chest as he smoothed her hair.

"You're safe," he whispered as he rocked her, just as he had through every nightmare since he had removed her from Wilburn's home. "We're here, Emilia. You're safe."

Her heart was still pounding but she stopped flailing and gripped her hands against his skin, trying to draw in breath as she fully exited the dream state and came back to reality. When she no longer felt like she had been racing at full speed, she drew back a little.

"I'm sorry," she whispered. "You have been so kind about these nightmares, but it must be trying."

He smoothed the tangles of her hair away from her forehead and kissed her gently. "Nothing about you has ever been trying, love. The only difficulty about the nightmares is that I hate to see you in such a state."

She swallowed hard and rested her head back in the crook of his shoulder. "You said *we're* here," she whispered. "But where is Wren?" She glanced at the windows and realized it was no longer light outside. "And why is it so dark?"

He smiled. "We came in to fetch you to bathe and found you fast asleep. So instead of waking you, Wren cleaned himself up and wrote the letters he talked about earlier."

"The ones to put Wilburn off our trail?" she asked, sitting up a little straighter. Now that she was coming out of the terror of her nightmares and the confusion of sleep, she was beginning to attend better.

Aiden nodded. "Then he went into the village to have them posted to the friends who will help with the subterfuge. He'll be back shortly."

"And did you bathe?" she asked.

"I did," he said softly, then lifted his gaze to hers almost conspiratorially. "In his bathwater."

She shivered at how erotic he made that sound. "Mmm, I wish I could have watched you both."

"We'll have plenty of time for that," Aiden assured her.

She smiled but she wasn't so certain of that. Her nightmare was closer to reality than she wanted to discuss at present. "And did you two…do anything together while I slept so innocently just a room away?" she asked, tracing his chest with her nails now.

He laughed, a low chuckle that was filled with heat. "There was a great deal of longing, but you know that if it's not all of us, it's none of us, Emilia." He blushed a little. "Except for kissing. We did do some kissing."

She smiled along with him. "To be fair, so did you and I. Oh, and I kissed him, too. I suppose we don't count kissing in that promise."

"Fair enough. But if the two of us are going to indulge in each other, it will be with you tangled with us. Or watching us. Or directing us."

She bit her lip. "Oh, directing you. That sounds wonderful."

Wren's voice interrupted them. "Then I'd suggest you take your own bath, my lady, which has been refreshed, it seems, while I was taking care of my business. Then we can grant your wish."

Both of them turned and found him leaning on the door frame of the bedroom. Wren had shed his jacket when he entered the cottage and was now rolling up his sleeves to the elbow as he watched them together. Both she and Aiden gave a shiver at the sight of those forearms that were deliciously corded with muscle, those hands that were so strong and firm when they touched and stroked.

She forced herself to focus and pushed the coverlet away. Of course she was naked after all their earlier passion and she still felt a need to cover herself, despite the utter trust she had in these men. She fought it, working to recall that she had nothing to fear from their heated gazes. Neither of them had ever thought worse of her somehow. She doubted they ever could. It was part of why it had been so easy to keep the love she'd always felt for them alive, despite their separation. They were the loves of her life. And that fact was so easy and lovely that she nearly cried with it.

Especially since she so pointedly knew that it might not matter in the end.

But she pushed that away and motioned her head to the adjoining chamber where Aiden had come from earlier. "I assume my tub awaits me through there."

"It does," Aiden said, and motioned her in that direction.

They followed as if they were her servants, but she couldn't help but laugh when she heard Wren grunt, "Jesus. Those hips."

She twitched said hips a little more out of playful teasing even though her cheeks heated with the compliment and its accompanying desire. She gasped as she entered the dressing room. There was a big brass tub along the wall under a small window and it steamed with fresh water scented with something floral and fresh. There were clean towels resting on a stool beside the bath and other soaps awaiting her. After the past few days, her muscles ached and she felt a sharp twinge of longing as she looked at the welcoming water.

"Don't just sit there making love to the bath with your eyes," Aiden said with a laugh as he took her hand to steady her. "Sink in."

She smiled at him and did just that, stepping over the edge and settling beneath the warmth. When he released her she sank a little lower and dunked her entire body, including her head, beneath the welcoming heat. When she surfaced, she slicked her hair back and then settled against the tub to watch Aiden and Wren.

They were both staring, mouths slightly agape, at her. "You two look like you've never seen a naked woman," she teased.

"Not enough of this naked woman," Wren corrected. "Only in our dreams until earlier today. I think I'd never get enough of seeing you like this."

"And we've always been of a mind," Aiden said as he removed

the towels and set them on a dressing table so he could take the stool beside her bath.

Wren laughed. "That we have. Always wanted the same thing, Aiden and I."

She took the washcloth draped over the tub edge and wetted it, then lathered it with soap. "Each other," she said. "And me."

Wren nodded and grabbed for the chair at the dressing table. He turned it so that the back was facing her and straddled it. "Did you *always* know that?"

"That you and Aiden wanted each other?" she asked. Aiden glanced at Wren and then both of them nodded. "I suppose we never really discussed it out loud, did we? It just…was." She thought back to those lazy days when they were just becoming aware of attraction. When their longtime friendship had begun to shift to something more. "I think I started to understand the looks you gave each other when I was…fifteen? And how if your hands brushed, they would linger. Just as they did with mine."

"Did you ever find it strange? Uncomfortable?" Aiden asked. "I doubt it's something discussed with governesses or female friends, after all."

"No," she agreed softly. "But I never thought it odd. It was always so right. The way you loved each other, wanted each other, only made our bond stronger. It never diminished it. And today, watching you touch each other…" She shivered despite the warmth of the water sloshing around her as she washed. "It was so powerful. I love to see it. I want to see more of it."

Wren reached out and his fingers brushed along Aiden's thigh. Emilia clenched her own thighs together against the pleasure of it. She reveled in how Aiden's breath caught.

"We can do that," Wren said softly. "If Wilburn had known about this place, I think he would have directed me here after you, since he believes I might betray you for his money. We'll be safe here, and I've doubly ensured that by paying some locals to inform me if anyone comes here asking about either of you. The letters I wrote and sent for the viscount's benefit will take some time to filter over to him. And the information I'm seeking in the meantime will also take a while and is being handled by my most trusted associates. It all means we have a few weeks where there will be little to do but wait. We can spend those weeks here."

"Together," Aiden breathed.

Tears filled Emilia's eyes at that thought. A few weeks with these two men? Being loved and loving them? Pretending they were together for life? "That sounds like heaven," she whispered.

"But Emilia," Wren continued, his dark blue gaze holding hers steady. "You've been through a great deal. If you don't want this…if it's too much and you only want to be safe, we would never ask for more. This is for you. Whatever you need and want."

Emilia stared from one of them to the other and her heart swelled with the love that had never died. "What I need and want is both of you. Like we were earlier, and more. What I want is to live in this beautiful bubble and indulge in everything I was denied since I was parted from you."

Aiden relaxed a little with a laugh. "Thank God. Then let me wash your hair and we'll retire back to the bedroom where you can do exactly what you told me you wanted earlier."

Wren cocked an eyebrow. "What did you want, Emilia?"

"To direct you two," she said with a wink toward him. "As you show me how much you want each other."

CHAPTER 6

Wren

By the time Emilia was finished with her bath, Wren was already hard. It was impossible not to be when he watched her touch herself beneath the water. When he watched Aiden touch her, even in the benign act of washing her hair or helping her dry off. Not that it *was* benign, not really. It was still an act of passion, but also an act of love.

He had known it when he rode here to find them, when he allowed their passion to overflow earlier in the day, but now it was even more clear: he would not escape this unscathed. He would be changed forever. He welcomed it, in truth. He didn't want to be the same. He wanted to be theirs.

They moved to the bedroom together and Emilia, still wrapped in one of the towels from her bath, took a place on the settee before the fire. She lounged back, letting her towel peel away from her thigh, Wren thought on purpose.

"Aiden says I may direct you," she said, her voice thick with seduction and desire.

"I don't think you've had control in a while," Wren said softly.

"So take it, angel. Take it and wrap us around that pretty finger. I'll do anything you like to him."

Aiden's pupils dilated and Wren could tell he wanted to touch him. Grab him. But he didn't. He, too, wanted to give Emilia this chance at the control she'd lost when she married a man who would use and hurt her.

She drew a shaky breath. "You don't know the multitude of wicked acts that just flashed through my mind when you promised me that. I hardly know where to begin. But...when Aiden took you in his mouth earlier, it excited me. I want you to do the same for him. So I can see it. Please."

Wren couldn't hold back a groan of excitement at the order. How many times had he imagined taking Aiden in his mouth? Or pictured him when he had some other man between his lips in some anonymous hell? Too many times to count. And now it would be real.

He was shaking as he grabbed the chair Aiden had watched from when they all first made love together. He slid it closer to Emilia and gave her a small smile over his shoulder. She was trembling, her hands trailing over her legs in the most arousing way.

"Sit," Wren ordered.

Aiden arched a brow, but his pupils dilated with the dominance. "As you say, Mr. Wren."

Wren felt the corner of his lips twitch with a smile, one that faded as Aiden sank down and slouched, spreading his legs out so he looked dissipated and more tempting than anything Wren had ever seen.

"What next, Emilia?" Aiden said softly.

She whimpered. "Wren, kneel before him."

She tossed a pillow from the settee toward him. Wren caught it without breaking eye contact with Aiden and dropped it with a thump between Aiden's feet. He leaned in, gripping the arms of the chair to support himself as he slowly dropped to his knees there. Aiden's breath was short, ragged as they stared at each other.

"Tell me what to do, Emilia," Wren whispered.

There was a long pause and Wren looked at her over his shoulder. She had pushed aside the towel entirely now and sat naked on the chair, her hand between her legs, playing lightly. "Unfasten his fall front," she murmured.

He nodded and returned his gaze to Aiden. "Is that what you want?"

"You know it is," Aiden ground out. "I want to watch you take me in your mouth. I want to feel you on me."

"Yes," Emilia said. "Take his cock out and enjoy it, Wren. Stroke it and lick it and suck it until he's begging you for release. Until I'm shaking with my own. Until you ache from it."

Wren somehow managed to keep from spending just from their combined verbal torture and placed his hands on Aiden's thighs. They were so thick and heavily corded with muscle that twitched beneath his palms. He'd seen Aiden's cock earlier when they pleasured Emilia together. But this would be different. Just for him.

He unfastened the buttons on the fawn trousers that were impossibly tight around Aiden's very hard cock and finally freed him from their confines. For a moment Wren could only stare. He liked sex. He took his pleasure when he needed to do so, despite his continued feelings for the two people with him presently in the hot, close room. But this moment felt like more than sex. It felt like sacrament.

He reached out and stroked his fingertip along the satin flesh of Aiden's cock and the other man's eyes came shut with a low groan. He lifted slightly, as if reaching for more, and Wren smiled. He knew a little about that. Earlier it had taken every ounce of control in his body not to simply fuck Aiden's throat until he spent in a wild, unruly burst of pleasure.

"Like this, Emilia?" he asked, closing his fist around Aiden's length. Without looking at her, he shifted so she could see better.

"Yes," she moaned, and he smiled up at Aiden, who watched her for a moment.

"She likes it," he grunted. "So do I, Wren. It's better than I ever dreamed."

Wren stroke him once, twice, before he said, "Good."

Then he didn't speak for a while. He only focused on the pleasure. He pumped Aiden's hard cock with firm pressure as he gazed up at him, loving how he shook and twitched with the touch. He wanted to do it all day, just tease him while he looked into his eyes and felt Emilia at his back, arching and groaning against her fingers.

"For God's sake, suck me," Aiden finally moaned, his knuckles whitening against edge of the chair as he gripped it.

Wren chuckled. "Can you see, Emilia?"

"Yes, yes, yes," she whimpered, her voice broken.

Wren bent his head and lightly licked just the head of Aiden's cock, and Aiden gasped out his name as his hands came into Wren's hair. He didn't resist when Aiden tugged closer, forcing him to take a little more into his mouth. He liked the wordless demand, liked the feel of Aiden's thick hardness stroking over his tongue. He took more of him, filling his mouth up, circling the length of him, slow and steady.

"Fuck," Aiden whimpered. "Fuck."

And so Wren did. He fucked him with his mouth, deeper and deeper, with slow, certain strokes and firm suction. He reveled in the act, in the salty taste of Aiden's skin as he became more excited, in the way he stopped breathing entirely. And then Aiden began to thrust even deeper and Wren was undone. The feel of him against the back of his throat, the way Aiden looked as Wren took him, the sound of Emilia's pleasure as she dragged herself closer and closer to completion was almost too much to bear.

And yet it was everything Wren had ever wanted in his wildest, wickedest fantasies. He wanted all of it and more. He never wanted it to end and he also wanted to end Aiden in the most explosive way, only to start all over until he was weak beneath Wren's tongue.

Aiden met his eyes and there was a sensuality there, an intent that matched his own. "You are so fucking good at that," he said, then he caught Wren's chin and tugged him off his knees to claim his mouth with a searing kiss. "But I want more."

"What is more?" Wren asked, hardly able to find words when his mind and body were rolling.

Aiden pointed over his shoulder toward Emilia and together they looked at her. She was shaking, and when both their attention was on her she arched, wetness coating her fingers as she came with a wailing cry that echoed in the room.

"Fucking hell," Wren said, his voice low and rough.

"Do you want us to fuck you, Emilia?" Aiden asked. "Back and forth, over and over until you are shattered?"

"Yes," she gasped out. "Please!"

Wren pushed to his feet and pivoted, grabbing Emilia's hand and tugging her to the bed. Aiden was already standing by the time he turned back, and he groaned as Wren pushed her down so she was bent over the high edge of the mattress, her fingernails scratching against the soft fabric of the coverlet as she waited. He didn't allow her to wait long.

He speared her body with his cock in one long thrust and she bucked against him, gripping him in her wet heat to the point where he could have spent right there. But that wasn't what he wanted. He took her a few times, then stepped back so Aiden could take his place. As he rolling his hips against her backside in a few heavy thrusts, he cupped the back of Wren's neck and kissed him.

She was arching and mewling now and the two men took advantage, taking her back and forth, kissing and touching in between, the pleasure between them so powerful that it was almost impossible to separate it all. Emilia's fingers went back to her clitoris, rubbing it as she was taken, and as Wren gripped her hips and slammed into her, she came. It was impossible to exit her body then. She milked him and he threw back his head with a long moan of pleasure. Then he came with her, filling her with his essence and his love and his desire until he felt weak with it.

They were both shaking as he withdrew from her wet body. He waited to Aiden to return to his place behind Emilia and take his pleasure, as well, but she seemed to have other ideas. She turned and grabbed Wren's hand.

"Finish what you started," she whimpered.

He understood, his heart rate increasing as he went back on his knees and took Aiden back in his mouth. He tasted of Emilia's pleasure now, sweet and sticky, salty and earthy all at once, and Wren sucked harder and faster to devour all of their combined flavors.

He felt Emilia's fingers come into his hair. She pressed against the back of his skull, taking control of his pace as he took Aiden closer to oblivion. When he looked up at them, he found Aiden kissing her, their tongues tangling wildly as he moaned out his pleasure into her mouth.

When he came, Wren took every drop, savoring it like fine wine until Aiden went soft against his tongue. Only then did he withdraw and stand to join in their kiss as the heat between them transformed from heady passion to something more gentle, more loving. They moved to the bed together, a tangle of arms and legs and kisses, and for a while they simply lay that way, silent in the face of pleasure and the power of their connection.

But Wren knew in his heart that very soon they would have to be far more than silent. They would have to work out the past, the present, and mostly the future.

Emilia

Emilia hadn't felt peace for so long that she hardly recognized it as she lay with her head on Wren's chest, his fingers tangling in her hair. Aiden rested his head on her hip, brushing his lips there from time to time even as his fingers played along the thick muscle of Wren's naked thigh. But this *was* peace. Not fear.

Not acceptance of a life she didn't want. Not anticipation of whatever horror would come next. Peace.

But it was an illusion. It *felt* real but if she tried to cling to it, she knew it would disappear. And worse still, it could destroy both these men. If it…and she…hadn't already.

And so she had to break the spell that had been woven so sweetly by passion and surrender.

"You wrote your letters to Wilburn, Aiden said earlier," she said softly, tracing the line of muscle on Wren's bicep.

He hesitated a moment and then looked down at her. His expression was now hooded, concerned. "Yes."

"Do you think he'll believe your false leads?" she asked. "That he'll truly leave us alone for weeks?"

He was quiet, like he was calculating, before he spoke. "Wilburn believes Aiden and I were rivals for you, so I doubt he would imagine the truth. And I…leaned into that idea in the letters. I think it will take time for him to become truly impatient and start to demand more action on my part."

"But you *will* take action on your part," Emilia said with a sigh that shuddered out. "Not against me, but for me. As much as we'd all like to do so, we can't stay in this cottage for the rest of our lives and pretend Wilburn and the world don't exist."

"No," Wren said, and she saw his gaze shift to Aiden. "As heavenly as that sounds, it isn't a solution."

"And nor is you going back to the viscount," Aiden added with a deep frown. "We'd never send you back to danger, Em."

"I know that," she said, and shut her eyes. "I seem to be the only one of the three of us willing to put the others in danger."

Now Wren sat up and it forced her to do the same. "Don't ever say that again, Emilia." His tone was sharp. "Ever. I'm glad you reached out to Aiden, I'm glad I was the one sent to pursue you two. I don't give a damn about the consequences. You mean too much to me. If that man had harmed you, I would have died, myself. Or at least tortured myself to my dying day that I had done nothing to save you."

"He's right," Aiden added. "I won't regret any consequences to helping you. I never could. I only wish we could have done so sooner."

Tears stung her eyes at their passionate defenses of her, even against her own self-loathing. "It's been so long since I had kindness, I almost forgot what it was like. Kindness and desire and pleasure and…and love." She looked to Wren and then Aiden. "You know I never stopped loving either of you."

Wren smiled a little, his normally serious expression brightening significantly. "I have ached to hear those words for years."

Aiden nodded. "We were too strongly bonded to stop the love between us. I always knew time and distance wouldn't be enough. And it hasn't been. I love you both as much as did all those years ago. Perhaps more, because I know what it's like to lose you."

"And I fear we'll all know it again, before this is over," Emilia said. She detangled herself from the two men and went down from the bed. She paced over to the window and peeked around the filmy curtain that protected them from the outside world and all its prying eyes and terrible concerns. Aiden's cottage was situated away from the village a few miles away, so there were no people, just green fields and a copse of trees in the distance.

"I know you're afraid." Emilia turned back to see that Wren had left the bed as well and he came toward her slowly, like she was a filly that could spook if he wasn't careful. "And after so long, I understand how it might feel hopeless. But let that go for now. We'll work out our next step, but that doesn't mean we can't enjoy what we're sharing here as we do."

She blinked. "More of…more of this?"

Aiden was sitting up in the bed. "Yes. You deserve that respite. We all do after so much time apart. Please, Emilia, don't run off into some terrible future before it comes. Stay here with us. Be with us. Trust us."

Wren looked back over his shoulder at him with a smile of adoration that warmed Emilia's heart. Trust them. Of course she did, even though she realized that trusting anyone was hard after so many years of only having herself to depend upon. But the idea of not having to protect herself was such a relief.

She nodded. "I want that. And I...I'll do my best not to let whatever the future may be ruin what is present. Ruin this."

Wren reached out and took her hand, drawing her forward against his chest where he folded her into his safe, warm arms. She relaxed against him, reveling in the smell of him, the feel of him.

"As much as I'd love to watch you two hold each other for the next hour," Aiden said, the smile in his voice recognizable even before Emilia looked at him and saw it brightening his face. "You need to eat. I'll make food."

Wren crooked his finger and Aiden's brown eyes dilated instantly. He got up and came to them. Wren tugged him into the embrace. And just before he kissed Emilia, then drew Aiden in to join them in that kiss, he whispered, "In a little while, love. In a little while."

CHAPTER 7

Aiden

Aiden stood at the fire in the kitchen, stirring a pot of stew over the flames. He didn't often cook for himself. He was a successful solicitor, he had servants, including a fine cook. As the son of a butler, he'd learned when he was a young man from other servants in Emilia's house, before success had allowed him luxuries. He actually found the act of cooking relaxing. When he was doing it for two people he loved? Even better.

The past two days with Wren and Emilia had made their earlier declarations of love to each other even more true. He *did* love them. And he was wracking his brain with some way they could be together, that they could save her from the fate so many women of her rank and position faced.

"You are frowning."

He turned from the pot and smiled slightly as Wren entered the kitchen. He wore trousers, but he was shirtless and that ripple of muscle and flesh was utterly distracting. Even more so since Aiden knew the flavor of his skin, the way he trembled when he came, the absolute control he had when he was focused on making Aiden or Emilia…or both of them…do the same.

"I'm focused," Aiden said, and returned his gaze to the stew, where he threw in a few herbs.

"On the food or the real problem?"

Aiden glanced at him again. "Both," he admitted. "Where is Emilia?"

"Sleeping." Wren frowned. "At least her nightmares have subsided, but her exhaustion is so plain. As if she hasn't had truly restful sleep in years."

Aiden sighed. "At least we can allow her that now. She knows she's safe here with us."

Wren took a seat at the table in the middle of the kitchen. Aiden had a wooden cutting board laid out there with a few carrots he intended to add closer to the end of cooking so they would retain crispness. Wren grasped the knife and began to cut them as they spoke.

"I expect we may receive a letter from her husband today, forwarded from a contact in London. If that happens, I intend to hide it from her."

Aiden hesitated before he stirred the pot. "Lie to her."

"No, protect her, as you said." Wren shook his head. "She doesn't need to know every vile thing that man will surely say. She has enough fear, I would spare her as much as I could."

"And yet you're angry that Emilia and I did just that same thing over the years with you," Aiden said softly.

Now it was Wren who hesitated in his cutting. He didn't look up. "That's different. I wasn't in danger from anything you two tried to protect me from."

"Weren't you?" Aiden said and now he faced Wren full on. "When your father died, you were much more vulnerable than I was."

"He was a man of affairs," Wren said carefully. "Technically more elevated than a butler."

"But you were on your own," Aiden insisted. "And thankfully you were taken in to train as an investigator, but we all know you could have been pushed out onto the street for any minor infraction at that point. Your position was precarious—please don't pretend it wasn't."

Wren's jaw tightened and now he did look up. "Fine."

"Emilia and I were so proud of you, watching you rise from those beginnings, study to become the fine investigator I know you to be now. Respected, Wren. Sought after. Successful. Would that have happened if Emilia's father...or more likely her husband's family, had declared some kind of vendetta against you for trying to interfere with her marriage?"

Wren let out a long sigh. "Of course not. They could have... likely would have...destroyed any chances I had at an occupation, even as a servant, if I failed at my training. It would have ruined me. But I regret it, regardless. Don't you?"

Aiden tapped the spoon on the edge of the pot and covered it, pulling it slightly away from the fire so it would stay hot but not cook quite so quickly. "I suppose you're talking about regretting not stepping in more strenuously to keep Emilia from marrying the viscount? Yes, of course I regret it, especially considering what I know now. But we said it then and it's not less true now, Wren. We had no power. You and I ultimately built that through sweat and hard work and sacrifice. And now that we have it, I think we can use it for her sake. For all our sakes."

Wren's brow wrinkled. "What are you suggesting?"

"Wouldn't you like our life to be like this forever?" Aiden moved toward him, stroked his fingers along Wren's shoulder, tracing the muscle there and loving the shiver Wren gave in response...the way his blue eyes dilated with emotion and desire in a potent mix. "To be together, all three of us, as we always should have been."

Wren caught his breath and his voice was wobbly as he said, "That sounds like a dream, not a reality."

"Because of our pasts?" Aiden pressed. "Because of Society's views? Because of your own fear?"

Wren shrugged. "All of those things, I suppose. You don't exactly see many people living that way." His expression flickered. "Though…"

"Though what?" Aiden asked, meeting his stare. "What are you thinking about?"

"I…it doesn't matter," Wren whispered.

"Why?"

"Because Emilia's husband is hellbent on getting her back and that's what I must focus on, even if we pretend this cottage is the whole world. I can't bear to…to hope for something more."

"Why?" Emilia's voice asked.

They both turned and found her standing at the entrance to the kitchen, one of their shirts pulled over her shoulders, her hair loosely bound. Aiden could hardly breathe, looking at how beautiful she was.

"Please don't worry yourself," Wren said, stepping away from Aiden and toward her.

"I will," Emilia said. "I'm not a fool, Wren. I hear your pain when you say something like you cannot bear to hope. I see it on your face. We've played and loved and pleasured in this wonderful house for days, but the one thing we haven't done is perhaps what is most painful and most necessary."

"And what is that?" Aiden asked when it was clear Wren couldn't make himself.

"Talked about our time apart."

"We did," Wren said, sending a side glance toward Aiden, as if he would save him. "We know now what you endured."

"Not me," she said softly, and took his hand, then reached for Aiden. "You. Both of you. We've avoided this subject, I think because it's painful and none of us wanted to ruin our wonderful reunion. But if I've learned anything over these years, it's that avoiding the truth will only lead to more sorrow. Please, I've been cut away from you both for so long. I want to hear what I missed as you both became the wonderful men you are now."

Aiden could see that Wren was uncomfortable by the way he shifted, that he wanted to escape this story, which made Aiden as curious as Emilia clearly was. He moved to cover their hands with his.

"I'll happily tell you about my life in the past years," he said. "Why don't we eat while we talk?"

"Yes," Emilia said, brightening at the thought. "I'd love that. The stew smells divine, Aiden."

He smiled as he returned to the fire and spooned stew into bowls for each of them and himself. They gathered utensils and moved out into the main room of the cottage to sit at the cozy table together. Aiden took a moment to take in the scene. The woman he loved wrapped in his shirt, the man he loved bare chested and beautiful as he poured wine for them all. There was such comfort in this, despite the years that had separated them. Such rightness.

And whatever Wren feared, whatever Emilia argued, Aiden didn't want to lose this. He would fight for it.

He lifted his chin. "You already know I started my journey to become a solicitor just after we were parted."

"Yes. You were apprenticed under Mr. Caldwell," Emilia said. "After your dear father's death."

"Thanks to your father's help," Aiden said softly.

Her cheek twitched. "My father made some very bad decisions in his years, but I always appreciated that he helped you both pay into training positions to rise above your fathers' places in his household."

"Yes," Wren said. "He was a complicated man."

"He was." She bent her head. "But please tell me about Caldwell, Aiden. Was he kind to you?"

Aiden shook his head. "I cannot believe you recall his name after all these years."

"I recall everything," she said softly, and smiled at him before she took a bite of stew and made a face of ecstasy that was distracting almost beyond measure.

"Yes, Mr. Caldwell very kindly took me under his wing and into his house, and after we three were parted I dove into my studies and work with even more gusto than I had done before. Soon I was doing half of the old man's work and then all of it as he got older and less able or interested. When he retired, he left his firm to me, as well as all his clients, including the estate of Emilia's father."

"You were good at the work," Wren said, a statement, not a question.

"Very," Aiden agreed. "That is not being cocksure, I know I'm good at what I do. I've worked on all kinds of contracts and disputes, and I don't have many unsatisfied clients. I've served everyone from country gentlemen all the way to the royal family of Athawick while they were here for their tour two years ago."

Both Emilia and Wren's eyes were wide. She clasped her hands together. "They made such a splash!"

"They did. And I've continued to do some work for them since, as they navigate the changes to their country. It has been, apart from thoughts of you two, a very good life."

"That was your business," Emilia encouraged. "But what about… personally?"

Aiden shifted and glanced at Wren. "Do you really want to know about my life after you two were gone?"

"Yes," Emilia said. "You know of mine. I want to know all your joys and sorrows. You never married, a fact I admit I'm selfishly happy about. But you must have had lovers. Perhaps even loves."

"Lovers," Aiden admitted. "Both woman and men in various arrangements over the years. But never loves. No, I never had any room in my heart for anyone else but the very people at this table."

Wren's nostrils flared a little and he stared at his hands, clenched on the tabletop before him, his food untouched so far. This subject clearly troubled him, though Aiden couldn't place why it would be so.

"Did you two ever see each other?" she asked. "The society of a successful barrister must be much the same as that of a well-thought of investigator."

"I only saw Wren twice in all that time," Aiden said softly. "Once at a club and once in the street. We didn't speak either time."

Her mouth twisted with sadness. "It is so unfair. Sometimes I liked to imagine that you two decided not to fulfill your unwanted promise to keep away from each other. That you found each other and were able to find comfort together."

"There was no comfort," Wren said, his voice rough.

She shifted her attention to him, as did Aiden. He still didn't understand Wren's expression. "Why do you look that way, Wren?" Aiden whispered.

Wren refused to meet his gaze. "Look like what?"

"Like it...hurts," Emilia said and she glanced at Aiden. He smiled at her despite it all. They were a united front now. "Why does it hurt still, Wren?"

He shifted and grabbed for his wine glass, downing the entirety in one rather ungentlemanly slug. When he had finished, he said, "Digging in the past won't change it, will it?"

Emilia reached out, cupping his cheek, smoothing her thumb along the rough stubble. Wren looked at her then, really looked at her, and their connection was so powerful that Aiden couldn't breathe. God, he could look at it forever.

"Please," she whispered. "There have been so many barriers between us, don't create another. Not now. Not after everything."

His eyes fluttered shut, his breathing grew more labored. Aiden could see his struggle, his heartache, and he ached in return. But he and Emilia sat quietly, simply waiting for Wren.

And at last he spoke. "Emilia, you said you never saw either of us again until you called for Aiden to help you. And Aiden, you said you only saw me twice in the years we've been parted. But...but it was different for me. I...I saw you both, many times. I watched you both, and it ripped me apart."

CHAPTER 8

Wren

After they were reunited, Wren had never intended to let Aiden or Emilia know the truth about the last seven years. It had hurt him enough that he didn't want to drag them into it. But he was, as he had always been, weak to them. And so he would hurt them and batter himself in the process, reliving moments that had burned like fire across his skin and had hollowed him out until he felt empty.

Aiden was staring at him, his eyes wide and his skin pale. "What…what does that mean?"

"Yes, please explain," Emilia said. She hadn't removed her hand from its place on his and she squeezed gently, offering support when he most needed it. He'd almost forgotten what it felt like.

"You wanted to know what our lives were like in the last seven years," Wren said softly. "I'll tell you and you might wish I hadn't. Yes, I became a successful investigator and I'm good at my work. I even enjoy it much of the time. People are puzzles and I am driven to solve those puzzles. And yet the tools I developed in my work stabbed me as often as they saved someone else."

He stopped talking for a moment as memories flashed through his mind. He must have shown it on his face because Aiden got up from the table and came to where Wren sat. His fingers threaded through Wren's hair, soft and gentle, and for a moment as he was touched by both of them, the world settled.

"The first time I used my skills to find one of you, it was accidental. I was researching the attendees of a ball for a case my mentor, Mr. Boyd, was investigating and I realized that Emilia and the viscount would be there. My world stopped as I stared at their names on the guestlist: Viscount and Viscountess Wilburn. All I could think was Emilia, Emilia…*my* Emilia."

He looked up and found Emilia's eyes had misted with tears. "It must have been a shock," she whispered.

He nodded. "It had been over a year since I last saw you at that point. I felt like I'd been riding at full speed and someone had ripped the horse from under me and I was just…falling. I had to fight to finish my work on that case and I promised myself I would forget it. Forget I'd seen your name, forget all the memories it stoked it me. But I couldn't. I'd find myself getting up at night, searching through documents on other cases, looking for your name. Looking for Aiden's."

Aiden's fingers stroked through his hair again and Wren let out a shuddering sigh. "You both became my obsession, as if no time had passed. I would do my work, of course I would. But at night I would use my resources to look into each of you. I didn't know about your unhappiness, Emilia, I swear to you I would have intervened earlier and bugger the consequences."

"Of course you didn't know," she said softly.

"But I knew when you were in London," he said. "I knew when your debts were paid at the milliners and the apothecary. I knew when Wilburn was out of town. You don't know how many times I rode past your house at those times, watching up at your windows as if I could see you. As if I could float up to you and steal a moment."

"Oh, Wren," she whispered, tears leaping to her eyes. For him. For her. For all of them.

"And you," he continued with a nod toward Aiden, who was now still as stone and just as unreadable with these confessions. "I knew about this cottage not because Wilburn asked me to chase you two down, but because I uncovered when it was gifted to you as payment for a contract you handled. I...I watched you. I knew which clubs you frequented. I even knew about your lovers. I would research them to ensure they wouldn't take advantage of you."

There was a long silence as both of them stared at him. He cleared his throat. "I violated your privacy, both of yours, many times. If you're angry about that, I deserve nothing less. And I apologize."

Emilia pushed back from the table and moved to him. Now he was buffeted on each side by his lovers. He had been before, in the passionate days and nights in the bedchamber. But this was different. They wrapped their arms around him, surrounding him with nothing but love.

Aiden leaned in, his mouth brushing Wren's cheek. "That must have been so painful."

He felt the pain keenly now and bent his head. A tear he couldn't control slid down his cheek, and Emilia brushed it away before she turned his face toward hers and lifted to kiss him gently. "I'm so sorry, Wren. I'm so sorry."

"The years went by with my nights filled with research of you. And during the day I worked for exactly the same kind of people who had taken my greatest loves from me," he continued, for he couldn't stop now. "With their pompous sneers and utter belief that they'd earned what they stole and hid and burned. I filled my coffers and hated myself."

"Look at me," Emilia said, cupping his cheeks and forcing him to do just that. "What you did to survive, to thrive, is not anything to be ashamed of. And if you did spy on us, then I know I, for one, don't judge you. If I had the resources, the freedom, I might have done the same, just to know you were both alive and well and moving through the world outside my window."

He leaned forward and pressed his forehead to hers. "You could offer me forgiveness?"

"I will always offer you forgiveness for any transgression, Wren. That is the way of love," she whispered.

"And what about you?" Wren asked, almost afraid to look at Aiden. He might have offered sympathy for the pain Wren had endured in his obsessive work to watch them, but that didn't mean he wasn't angry.

"What you did, I longed to do," Aiden said softly. "But I was too cowardly. So I can't judge you, only marvel at how strong you were. And be glad that you were my unseen guardian angel."

"Did you ever give yourself time for pleasure?" Emilia asked. "For joy?"

She was asking about lovers, Wren supposed. About moments were he might lose himself the way he lost himself here with them. He cleared his throat. "I was no monk," he admitted. "But I never saw my dalliances as anything more than a way to purge a physical need when it hit a peak and distracted me from my cases. I had little heart for anything else."

Emilia's pity was clear on her face as she cupped his cheek. "Then you have earned every pleasure you denied yourself over the long years, Wren. And if you'd come back to the bedroom, I hope you would let Aiden and I give you what you missed. What we all missed. Please?"

He was trembling as he looked back and forth between the two loves of his life. How he needed them. How he so desperately didn't want to lose them again. And if he might, then he wanted to make the most of the time they had left before they had to make decisions about a foggy future fraught with danger.

"Yes," he murmured, and it was Aiden who pulled him in for a hungry, heated kiss. He surrendered himself to it, to the flavor of his man, to the feel of his fingers digging into Wren's bare back even as Emilia kissed a heated trail along his shoulders.

They moved together, just as they had that first day, back into the bedroom where they had shared so much over the past few days. It always felt like coming home to Wren, but now it felt like something more. As Aiden unfastened his trousers and Emilia reached around to stroke his hardness, their wonderful attention fully focused on him, and he realized that they were freeing him. From the past, from the pain, from everything but them.

He moaned as pleasure streaked up his cock, powerful and wild as Aiden joined in the gentle stroking of his shaft. Emilia's fingers tangled with his and she whimpered as her teeth scraped the flesh of Wren's shoulder.

"We have had you together, Emilia. Does it make you feel loved?" Aiden whispered, sucking and swirling his tongue around a spot at the base of Wren's throat that drove him wild between each word.

She nodded. "Yes. It makes me feel complete."

"I want to do that for Wren."

Emilia's eyes widened. and Wren watched as his two lovers' gazes met over him and she smiled.

"Would you like that, Wren?" she asked softly, seductively.

Wren nodded, fully surrendering to this and to them and feeling the warmth of that wash over him and take away all the agony his life of responsibility and loss had created in his chest.

"Lie back," Emilia urged him, pressing him toward the bed as Aiden pulled away and went digging in drawers for the familiar bottle of slick oil that they used to ready Emilia so many times since their reunion.

"Have you done this before?" Aiden asked as he returned to Wren, climbed onto the bed at his feet and spread his legs slightly so he could ease closer. His palm cupped Wren's calf and it felt like his skin was alive as he arched with a hiss of pleasure.

"Had a man in my arse?" Wren gasped out. "Y-yes."

"Good," Aiden said, licking his lips. He motioned his head toward Emilia. "Suck him, let me see you ready him for you."

She nodded and smiled at Wren. "I love to have you in my mouth, you know. I used to dream of it."

Those words were as powerful as any touch and Wren let out a garbled groan before he caught her hand and drew her across him. He kissed her, deep and slow, tasting every inch of her mouth until she was whimpering and moaning his name.

"I want you to straddle my mouth while you lick me," he murmured as he let her part from him. "Do you understand?"

Her pupils dilated as what he desired became clear and she moved fully onto the bed. Aiden hadn't moved as he watched them together, almost like he was frozen with the images of their passion. But when she straddled Wren's shoulders, Aiden at last leaned in to kiss her over Wren's hard cock.

"Fuck his mouth, Emilia. Come all over him so I can taste you later," Aiden ordered, his voice suddenly harder, more in control.

She responded by catching Wren's cock and stroking him again. Wren gasped and gripped her hips, looking up at the gorgeous, wet pussy poised over him. He could scent her excitement and it only encouraged his own, and just as she covered him with her mouth, he licked her.

They both jolted at the feel of the other and he smiled against her as he gave in to the heated pleasure of what they were doing. She thrust her mouth over him, eager and hungry, taking him all the way to her throat before withdrawing and smothering him in perfect suction and wetness. He responded by devouring her with all the enthusiasm he felt for the act, tasting her and teasing her, fucking her with his tongue and sucking her clitoris until she was rolling her hips over him and chasing the high of release that he could already feel coming by the way her thighs shook and gripped around him.

And just when it couldn't get better, just when he was lost to the bliss, Aiden finally parted his legs, tilted his arse up, and began to circle the tight hole there with his fingers.

Wren came without warning, pushing his hips so hard that he feared he could hurt Emilia, but she only gripped him tighter, taking every drop of his release and continuing the sucks and licks as Aiden thrust his finger, then another, then a third into the place where he would take Wren. Claim him.

Emilia rocked her hips back and only then did her mouth leave his cock. She cried out, her pussy flooding with release and rippling against his tongue as she swore and moaned and shook with her own orgasm. He collapsed against the pillows, still twitching as she stroked him absently with her hand and Aiden continued to ready him with his fingers.

Wren knew his night had thankfully only just begun. He couldn't wait for everything that would come next.

CHAPTER 9

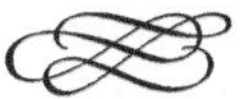

Emilia

Emilia had come many times with these men, but this time felt different. With Wren's mouth buried against her body, as she watched Aiden gently ready him with his thick fingers and she sucked him to release, she felt…wicked. She felt worshiped and adored. And she felt powerful. After all, she was in control of this as much as either of them. They gave her that gift.

She lifted herself up and scooted down Wren's body, now straddling his hips as she leaned up to kiss Aiden as he continued to finger Wren. Aiden moaned against her mouth.

"I can taste him," he whimpered.

She smiled and then said, "He's still hard."

"Oh yes, I see that, angel," Aiden said. "Will you ride him for me? Make him fill you up so I can see him overflowing from you?"

She shivered at the wicked images and looked back over her shoulder at Wren. He'd moved up to his elbows and he was hardly breathing as he watched her shift, lifting up, gripping his somehow still-hard cock and rub it against her dripping body. When she took him in a hard, slick stroke, he bucked beneath her and swore.

Aiden smiled. "When a man comes, he's so sensitive, Emilia. Imagine how much you're torturing him, pleasuring him as you ride him. As you use him."

She began to rock over him, lifting her hands to press them to Aiden's chest, their eyes meeting. "I want to watch you fuck him, too," she whispered, shocked at how bold these men made her.

Aiden nodded, his smile fading, his expression turning wild and wicked. He caught her hand and poured a little of the oil over her palm and fingers, then set the bottle aside as she gripped his cock. She rolled her hips over Wren again and again even as she stroked Aiden with her fist, watching his head dip back against his shoulders, his mouth open to expel a shaky breath.

Wren lifted beneath her and she gasped, herself, lost in the sensation of him for a moment. Aiden smiled at him over her shoulder and then withdrew from her palm and positioned himself at the arse he had been preparing. "Ready?" he asked, and Emilia knew it wasn't her he was asking.

"Yes." Wren's voice was garbled and harsh behind her, and he stopped breathing entirely as Aiden pressed himself at the entrance and then moved forward.

Emilia held still and watched, knowing exactly how good this man felt when he took her just like this. When he stretched her arse while she was being taken by another. She knew exactly how full and achy Wren had to be.

Aiden's fingers came into her hair and he kissed her hard and deep as together they began to move against Wren. He was moaning and arching beneath them both, and they became one organism, seeking pleasure, unaware of anything else in the world but each other and the pleasure they created.

"Come for me," Aiden whispered against her lips.

She was so close to the edge, his request wasn't hard to honor. She ground down against Wren faster, her legs shaking, her brow sweaty with exertion and sensation. The pleasure built, curling through her entire being, and then the waves hit and she cried out, clinging to Aiden as he increased his own pace. Wren was incoherent now, moaning out his own pleasure. He came as her orgasm began to fade, filling her while Aiden gripped his fingers against her hips and did the same to him.

His kiss deepened, slowed, and Wren sat up behind her, his arms coming around her stomach, his mouth against her shoulder. "God, that was everything."

She nodded as she broke Aiden's kiss. "Everything," she repeated as she traced his cheek with a finger and then turned her head so she could kiss Wren.

Slowly they all parted, and Aiden fetched damp cloths so they could carefully clean themselves up from the sticky results of the passion they'd shared. Then they collapsed on the bed together, legs tangled and mouths seeking as the warmth of pleasure and love settled into the quiet room. Emilia was floating off to sleep when there was the sound of the bell ringing from the other room.

She felt Wren stiffen and she opened one eye to see him staring at Aiden. There was silent communication that went between them, something secret that she didn't understand, and immediately she went on alert as Wren slipped from the bed and threw Aiden's dressing gown over his gorgeous, naked form.

Without a word, he exited the room and shut the door behind him. She heard the door outside open, heard Wren's voice though she didn't understand the words, and another voice respond. Then the door shut. Even after a few moments, Wren didn't return, and she looked up at Aiden. His expression was pinched and worried.

"What are you two hiding?" she asked.

Aiden glanced down at her sharply. "Nothing."

She sat up now and shook her head. "Sweetest Aiden, do you forget that I know you two? I can see when you're lying. What is it?"

"Nothing to trouble yourself about. Is that better?" he asked. "Let Wren take care of—"

He didn't get to finish the sentence. Emilia got up and without dressing left the room and entered the main chamber of the cottage. Wren was sitting at the desk in the corner, bent over a letter.

"What are you hiding from me?" she asked without preamble.

Wren's gaze jerked up and he set the letter face down so she couldn't see, which did nothing to make her less certain that it was about her. She folded her arms across her bare breasts and shook her head.

"Have we not hidden enough from each other in the attempt to protect ourselves? Have we not gone through enough and become enough to each other now to trust that we are stronger *together*?"

She felt Aiden at her back, then his hand came to cup her hip. "She's right," he said softly. "She's right, Wren."

For a moment, Wren was frozen, staring at the two of them. Emilia could practically see him working through all the answers, all the arguments. But at last, he bent his head slightly and then got up and came across the room to her, the letter in hand.

"It's from the viscount," he said softly. "In answer to a message I had posted from London by a fellow investigator I trust implicitly, Derrick Huntington. I also asked him to do a bit of looking into the viscount's activities, so there is also a note from him in the pages behind the viscount's." He hesitated and didn't offer her the heavy vellum sheets yet. "Emilia, what you read will be troubling. I...I hesitate to hurt you."

She gritted her teeth as she held out a hand. "I already know my husband's disdain for me and I suspect far darker motives to his actions. I need to see this. I need to know where I stand."

Wren cleared his throat and looked at Aiden. "Then let's get you something to put on and we can sit together and look at this. And decide what our next move is."

"Yes," Aiden said softly. "We'll be with you, Emilia, no matter what."

She nodded but from Wren's pale expression and Aiden's dire tone, she was beginning to fear what she would read more and more. Because she knew, perhaps better than either of them, that what was about to happen could change everything. What she was about to read could tear them all apart.

Wren

Wren had put on his trousers, Aiden had done the same and Emilia had taken Aiden's dressing gown and wrapped it around herself. Wren might have wondered at how erotic she could look in a garment two sizes too big for her frame, but at that moment, he couldn't focus on something so pleasurable.

All he could see was Aiden's drawn, worried expression as they sat together on the settee by the fire and Wren finally handed over the letters that had drawn them away from fantasy. Permanently, he feared.

"Shall I read them out loud?" Emilia asked. "So Aiden will know and Wren can hear the words again?"

"Please," Aiden said as he covered her shaking knee with his hand to steady her.

She glanced at him in thanks and then cleared her throat. "The first is from Wilburn. He writes, *I am disappointed to find that you are still in London, Mr. Wren, though I suppose you must exhaust all closest ties before you go farther. But I expect results as you head to Kent.*" She cut herself off. "Why did you tell him Kent?"

Wren shrugged though he felt anything but nonchalant about this conversation. "Because it's in the opposite direction from here."

She blinked for a moment and her cheeks paled. "Because… because you think he might send someone else after us?"

He didn't respond for a moment as he tried to find a way to keep her calm. At last Aiden filled the space. "He's right to be careful, isn't he?"

She nodded and bent her head. "Yes." Her breath was shaky a moment and then she continued to read. "*Your question about my wife's relations is a good one. As difficult as she is, she has not kept the favor of her cousins or friends over the years, so I doubt she has anywhere to run to. A point in our favor. I'll look for your next letter in a few days. Wilburn."*

Her lips were pressed hard together as she set the page away. "He *kept* me from my cousins and friends," she said through gritted teeth.

"I'm sure he did," Aiden soothed softly. "Isolating you was in his best interest."

Wren was pulsing with rage, but he refused to show it and take away from Emilia's pain by forcing her to soothe or comfort him. "And his belief that you are friendless is in ours. He doesn't seem to suspect anything still about our true relationship to each other. But...but if you look at that next page from Huntington, you'll see that things have still taken a turn."

He hated that Emilia's hands began to shake as she lifted the next page in the letter. Unlike the viscount, whose handwriting was flowing and overdone, Huntington's was more sharp and crisp. Rather like the man himself.

"I include the viscount's response to the letter you had me post here in London and also send a report from what I've been looking into. I fear you were right to worry, old friend. It seems the viscount has looked into other ways of finishing this domestic issue with your friend. He was overheard seeking less than savory characters willing to take care of her—"

Emilia broke off with a cry and pushed to her feet, the letter fluttering to the floor as she paced away, her shoulders shaking with emotion. When Wren began to get up to follow her, she held up a hand and waved him back. She stood at the fire, her head bent.

Aiden swallowed hard and reached out to touch Wren's arm before he swept up the page she had dropped and continued reading from where she had become overwhelmed. *"He was overheard seeking less than savory characters willing to take care of her with violence."* Aiden's jaw twitched, but he continued, *"Immediately I sent in my partner, Barber, to offer his services so that another criminal wouldn't take charge and create actual danger. Barber has convinced him he's the one for the job and for now we don't have any intelligence that he has hired anyone else to do the same. Please respond to me as quickly as possible and let me know your next desired step."* Aiden balled the paper up and threw it to the floor. "And then he signs it. Bloody hell."

Wren nodded. "Although there was no doubt earlier based on what you experienced, I think we have fulsome proof now that Wilburn intended and still intends to end your life, Emilia."

Her breathing became steadier and she turned. Wren's heart broke at the emptiness that was back in her stare. She had become so much more alive in the days the three of them had spent together where the hours of pleasure had let her forget fear and pain. But that was over now. He could see it by the set of her jaw.

"Yes. And there will be little we can do about it. Wilburn is powerful and influential. I'm certain he has left no trail of proof of his intentions toward me, so there will be no way to involve anyone to help in an official capacity. There is only one answer, though I suppose I always knew it."

Wren tilted his head. "And what is that?"

"I must leave the country. There is nothing else to do but start anew. And I must do it...I must do it alone."

CHAPTER 10

Emilia

If the circumstances she found herself in were not so dire, Emilia might have laughed at the response of her two lovers when she declared she would flee without them. Both men leapt to their feet, talking over each other, gesturing wildly. How she loved them both for desiring to save her. But because she loved them, she couldn't let them do that.

"*Please*," she said sharply, and their arguments stopped at her tone, which she gentled. "Please. I know you both feel a desire to help me. But to do so would be a sacrifice of yourselves. Wren, you have built a large clientele of influential and powerful people who come to you. And Aiden, you're a sought-after barrister. If you took me as your responsibility and fled, you would both lose everything. And Wilburn would do everything in his power to discredit your names far and wide even if he couldn't find us."

"Do you think that matters to us?" Aiden asked.

"It matters to *me*," Emilia said softly. "I would be brokenhearted if I knew I'd destroyed what you both worked so hard to create. That was never what I wanted for you two."

"Emilia," Wren said, crossing to her, catching her hands in his. "We've said it so many times to each other since being reunited, but it seems you need to hear it again. Aiden and I *love* you. We love you and being together again is like magic. We won't lose it again."

"But magic disappears on the wind, it's not…it can't be real," she whispered, and it broke her already broken heart to do so, especially when both men flinched. "Please, Wren, Aiden, don't…don't make this harder than it must be. Let me go. Let me go and move on with your lives so that I know that you two were still…together. Were still prosperous."

She could see Wren wanted to argue and he opened his mouth to do so, but Aiden stepped up. He pressed a hand to Wren's bare forearm. "Wren," he said softly. "If this is what Emilia wants, we can't force her to live the life we would choose for her."

Emilia almost collapsed in relief at Aiden's final acceptance of the way things had to be. But Wren stared at him, his expression a mix of betrayal and heartbreak. "You can't mean that."

"I do," Aiden said quietly, then he turned to Emilia. "If Wilburn is preparing something worse than he's already done, we must move swiftly in your escape from the country. Go get dressed, love. And Wren and I will work on a plan together."

She smiled at him, grateful on some level that he could be calm when she needed him to be. Even if it resulted in such pain. Hers, as well as theirs. But if there was one thing she had learned in the years since she'd first lost these two, life was sometimes pain. And at least this time she would have wonderful memories when they were parted.

She could only hope that would be enough.

Aiden

A iden felt Wren's anger toward him pulsing like a heartbeat, but he said nothing until Emilia slipped into the bedchamber and quietly closed the door behind her. Wren pivoted then and speared Aiden with a glare.

"What the fuck are you doing? How could you tell her that she should leave without us after everything we've been to each other these past few days?" Wren asked in an angry whisper so that she wouldn't hear their argument.

For a moment Aiden only looked at him, taken in, as always, by the beauty of this man's face, even in anger. His dark blue eyes were alive with the emotion, his hands trembled at his sides and there was a flush to his cheeks that was very like the flush that spread there when he was at the heights of pleasure. And oh, how Aiden loved him.

"Look at me," Aiden said.

"I am!" Wren snapped back, folding his arms across his chest.

Aiden moved forward and placed a hand on Wren's forearm, just as he had done earlier when they were talking to Emilia. He looked up into Wren's eyes. "No. *Look* at me. *See* me. Do you really think I want to let her leave? That I believe that's truly the answer?"

Wren took a shaky breath and his expression softened as he stared at Aiden. "No. I know you don't. I know."

"And she doesn't want to part from us, either. She wants to protect us from what she thinks is a hopeless situation. From destroying us."

"Yes," Wren said. "Because she is her. And she's perfect."

Aiden nodded. "She's spent the last seven years without any control. Without any hope. I don't want to be another man who takes that from her. Do you?"

"No." It was said with no hesitation. "But if you don't want this to end this way, what are you truly proposing?"

"We need to help her see that this *isn't* hopeless. That leaving... leaving together...is the start of something new and wonderful, not the end of it. That we'll survive it in every way that's meaningful and get to start the life that we should have always been able to lead together."

Wren stared at him for a moment and then his hands came up to cup Aiden's face. For that moment, there was nothing else in the world but the two of them and the way Wren's mouth lowered down toward his. They kissed, at first gentle, loving. Then with more passion as their tongues tangled and Wren's fingers slid into his hair.

When they parted, Aiden was a little dizzy and leaned on Wren with a smile. "The things you do to me."

"Nothing more than what you do to me," Wren said, and pressed his forehead to Aiden's gently. "So, my brilliant Aiden, what is your suggestion? Lead me into whatever plan you're formulating in your head to keep Emilia safe and allow us to be together."

Aiden kissed him once more and then backed away so he could actually think. "The best place we could go is Athawick."

"You mentioned it before, when you spoke of what you've done during our time apart. It's an island country, yes?" Wren said.

"Yes." Aiden smiled. "Have you ever been?"

"No," Wren admitted.

"I have. I attended with the Prince and his entourage during a tour there, as well as helped with some of the business arrangements between the two countries when the royal family came here."

Wren's eyes went wide. "By God, you *have* built yourself up. Why didn't I know this in my research?"

"Because the matter was very sensitive, I suppose," Aiden said. "And it was secret, so not even such a curious mind as yours could uncover it."

Wren smiled at him. "I'm proud of you."

Aiden felt himself blushing at that soft, yet powerful compliment coming from the lips of one of the only two people whose opinion actually mattered. "Thank you. The whole time I was there, enjoying the beautiful beaches and wonderful villages and people, I wished you and Emilia were with me. I could so easily picture us living in one of the colorful houses there, cozy and happy."

"And you have connections there," Wren said. "Powerful ones."

"I enjoy a sporadic correspondence with the current king. He was Prince Grantham when I visited and we worked closely together during our time. He is transitioning his government to a democracy, if you can believe it."

Wren's eyebrows went up. "I see. How egalitarian of him."

"He truly is." Aiden smiled. "And not terrible to look at either."

"Don't make me jealous," Wren said, but he was teasing if the brightness in his eyes was any indication.

"Not as handsome as you, I promise," Aiden said. "He's occasionally asked me for my assistance and has extended an invitation for me to visit many times, so we would be welcome there. Protected. And if we went, there would be other advantages."

"Such as?" Wren asked.

"Athawick is well known for its more…shall we say, *liberal* view of love and sex," Aiden said. "Three lovers living together might not be common even there, but it will surely meet with more acceptance. We could live in the open, unlike here or in the former colonies or on the continent."

Wren swallowed hard. "Live openly," he repeated. "I…I never thought…"

"I know. But it's possible."

Wren was silent for a long moment. "Then Athawick it is."

"Good," Aiden said with a sigh of relief, but also worry. "I only hope we can make it there. We would have to sail from London. And it's clear from what Huntington told us in his letter that Wilburn is still on the hunt for Emilia. Returning could be very dangerous and sailing even more so."

Wren nodded. "If you can provide us with the spot to go, perhaps I can help with the protection and cover."

Aiden tilted his head. "How?"

He was surprised that Wren's lips quirked a little. "I have

connections, too, my love. Just ones that are a little different than your own."

Aiden arched a brow. He wasn't accustomed to this tone from Wren. "Why do I feel like you're going to take us into a lion's den?"

Wren tilted his head back and laughed. "Well, perhaps it is that. But I think the lions I have in mind might be just the weapon we need."

Aiden still wasn't certain he liked the idea of lions, but asked no further questions. "I trust you. Just let me know where we need to go. I can arrange the transport."

Wren reached for him and tugged him in, folding his strong arms around Aiden and holding him tight. Aiden relaxed into his warmth, his strength and realized how much he had needed this over the years. How happy he was to have this man back in his life and his arms.

And now they just had to convince Emilia that she, too, belonged with them. That their love was a risk worth taking and a future worth grabbing.

CHAPTER 11

Wren

Wren looked out the carriage window as the edge of London grew up around them. He didn't like returning to the city with Aiden and Emilia before he was certain that he could keep them both safe, but there was little choice in the matter.

"Your leg is bouncing," Emilia said, reaching across the gap between the benches and laying a gentle hand on said knee.

He shook his head. "My apologies, I didn't even realize I was doing it."

"No apologies necessary," Aiden said, watching him just as closely as Emilia was. "You're obviously nervous, though. And you've been very secretive about just who we're going to meet."

Wren bent his head. "Yes, I realize I've been so the last few days. I'm sure it must not add to either of your sense of safety. I almost don't know what to say about the people we're putting our faith into."

"How long until we reach out destination?" Aiden asked.

Wren looked out the window again. "Perhaps half an hour, a little more if the carriage traffic is heavy."

"Then why don't you tell us a bit now?" Emilia said gently. "I admit I'd feel more secure if I knew something of where we're going here in London, so close to Wilburn and his obsessive hatred."

Wren nodded. "Of course. Let me see, where to begin. You two know that I have developed a bit of a reputation when it comes to investigating discreetly for the titled and rich."

Emilia nodded. "Yes."

"Sometimes I'm looking into a wayward spouse's affair, sometimes the activities of an estate manager who is skimming funds from a gentleman. But sometimes I look into deeper crimes. Especially when the victim in question doesn't want the public scrutiny of the guard's involvement. And *that* is how I met the people we're going to see today."

"So, they were victims of a crime," Aiden said softly.

"No." Wren drew a long breath. "They were the…perpetrators. Well, two of them were."

Emilia's eyes went wide. "What? You are taking us to meet criminals?"

"You sound almost excited," Wren said with a slight laugh at her bright-eyed shock.

"I admit, I don't think I've ever met a criminal."

"You lived with one," Aiden muttered, resulting in Emilia taking his hand and squeezing. "Wren, do continue."

Wren nodded. "They stole something from a very important person." He flinched. "Well, he thinks he's important, but he's actually just very pompous. At any rate, I was hired to return the item and bring the perpetrators to justice. Only when I found them, they were with a man who was driven to protect them. I realized there was…much more going on there. And I didn't fulfill my duty. Oh, I returned the item, but I had no intention of bringing the thieves to justice."

"Why?" Aiden asked.

Wren closed his eyes, flashing back to all those months ago, when he'd stood on the parlor of Richard Fitzroy and realized that the man was in love with the two thieves. That they had formed a life together. And that Wren couldn't break apart something he, himself, understood and longed for.

"They're like us," he said softly.

"You mean they're..." Emilia swallowed. "These three people are in love?"

Wren nodded. "And I couldn't trade that for a rich man's ego. We already suffered that fate ourselves. So I let them go."

"And you think that with their past as criminals they could help Emilia escape England without the viscount discovering her?" Aiden asked.

"Yes." Wren shuddered. "At least I hope they will."

The carriage pulled into the drive of a fine home and a footman from the estate hurried to open the door for them. Wren glanced at Aiden and Emilia, still close together, her hand trembling in his. He wasn't sure what was going to happen when they announced themselves to the inhabitants of this home. He could only hope it would be something good.

He exited the carriage first and didn't wait for them to follow as he strode up to where a butler was waiting. "Good afternoon, sir."

"Good afternoon," Wren replied as he withdrew a card from his jacket pocket. "Will you please advise Mr. Fitzroy that Mr. Wren is here to see him? And tell him it isn't on official business."

The butler's eyebrows raised slightly, but he motioned Wren and his companions into the house and to a parlor just off the foyer to wait while he ascertained if Fitzroy would see them. Emilia sat and Aiden took a place beside her, but Wren could only pace the room.

He moved to the fire and found on the mantel a miniature of a woman with loosely bound blonde hair looking over her shoulder with a wicked little smile. Zara Cooper. So at least Wren knew there was a still a bond between Fitzroy and the lady. He had a suspicion that meant Peregrine Huxley was also still in play.

The door behind them opened and Wren watched as Richard

Fitzroy entered the chamber. He was a very attractive man, with intense eyes and a full mouth. "Mr. Wren," he said with caution heavy in his tone. Then he glanced at Aiden and Emilia as they stood to greet him. "And you've brought friends."

"Yes," Wren said, moving forward with a hand outstretched. "I-I'm sorry I didn't send word first, it was poorly done of me. But I feared after our last encounter that you might not see me."

Fitzroy was staring at him intently as he shook his hand. "At our last encounter you were nothing but a friend. I'm happy to receive you, assuming you didn't lie to my butler and you aren't here on official business when it comes to…to the people I care about."

"No," Wren hastened to say. "I come entirely of my own volition. In fact, I come seeking your aid and the aid of those very friends if they'll allow it." He cleared his throat. "But first let me introduce my friends. This is Mr. Edwards and Viscountess Wilburn. They are my dearest friends. My most…my most *beloved* friends."

Fitzroy's nostrils flared slightly as he looked Aiden and Emilia up and down. Then he smiled slightly. "Good afternoon to you both. I am pleased to meet you, especially since Hux will owe me a pound."

"I beg your pardon?" Wren asked.

"When you came into our lives last year, I told Zara and Hux that I thought you understood our arrangement far more intimately than the average person might have. And Hux especially denied that it could be true. He was willing to place a wager on that fact, and I assumed it would remain outstanding for the rest of our days, but now that you are here with your *beloved* friends, it seems I will collect."

Wren glanced at Aiden and Emilia, hoping his expression let them know he was there for them. "You shall, for you are correct that I did understand you then. And even better now."

"Then what is it you need from me? From Hux and Zara?"

Wren clenched and unclenched his hands at his sides. "When I came to you, I offered assistance because I *did* understand the desire to protect someone you loved, especially against another who had more power and might use it to destroy them. Now I find myself in the same position, trying to protect Lady Wilburn—"

"Oh, please don't call me that," Emilia said softly, which drew Fitzroy's attention back to her swiftly.

"Emilia," Wren corrected. "Aiden and I need to protect Emilia and we may not be able to do it in a lawful way."

"And you think two criminal masterminds may have some advice on that matter?" Fitzroy said with a tilt of his head.

"Please," Wren said at just above a whisper because he couldn't force himself to be any louder when his entire being felt like it was going to shake down to nothing.

Fitzroy looked over the three of them for a brief moment and then nodded. "I'll fetch the others. They can make their own decisions about assisting you. Please, make yourselves drinks while you wait." He motioned to the sideboard and then departed the room.

Wren sagged with relief. The first step had been made and now his hope was growing. Aiden got up and moved to fix the drinks that had been offered while Emilia stepped up to Wren and slipped her hand into the crook of his arm as she rested her head against his chest.

"Is it wise to reveal so much?" she asked. "Even if it sounds like these three people are like us?"

He shrugged. "I must offer vulnerability to be trustworthy to these three, I think. I'm sorry if it is a humiliation."

She lifted her head and touched his cheek. "I'm proud of who I love, Wren. There's no humiliation."

He smiled at her and then bent his head to gently kiss her just as the door to the chamber opened again and Fitzroy returned, this time with Zara Cooper and Peregrine Huxley behind him. He heard Emilia catch her breath and couldn't blame her. The three of them were stunning together. Zara was a true beauty and Huxley was very tall, Wren had forgotten how tall, with curly salt-and-pepper hair and an olive complexion. Certainty all but poured from him. He was not a man to be trifled with.

"You remember Mr. Wren, loves," Richard said. "Even though when you last met him you were both in disguise."

"I remember he did us a kindness," Zara said as she nodded toward him. "One it seems he might wish to have repaid if Richard's brief description is correct. But first, let us meet your...*beloved friends.*"

Wren briefly introduced Emilia and Aiden and was surprised by how much warmth they were met with. The last time he'd encountered these three, there had been fear to all of them. Hopelessness. Now they seemed at peace together. Joyful. Safe.

He knew how the tables had turned. He and Aiden and Emilia were the fearful ones now. But this gave him even more hope for the future because if they could make it with all the obstacles that had been in their way, he knew he and his lovers could survive and thrive, as well.

"Please sit," Zara said, and motioned to the settee where Aiden and Emilia had first sat together. They returned to that place, but Wren only moved to stand behind them, placing a hand on each of their shoulders.

Huxley arched a brow at the action and then reached into his pocket to toss Richard a few coins. "You can collect the rest of the wager later," he said, quirking his lips. "For now, why don't you three tell us why you're here? And why her ladyship looks so fearful."

Wren squeezed Emilia's shoulder gently and drew a breath to begin, but she reached up to cover his hand and looked up at him. "It's my story. I should tell it. I should ask for the help myself."

Aiden made a soft sound in his throat and settled his hand on her knee. Together they buoyed her up as she softly told the story of their parting, of her marriage, of the attempt on her life by her husband and at last how she had fled with Aiden and ultimately came to be with both of them. When she was finished, her shoulders were trembling. Wren had never been so proud of her, to open herself up in such a way. He knew it was difficult, and also an act of trust toward *him*. It meant the world.

"As you can see, I need to flee for my life," she said at last.

Zara's expression had softened with every word and now she scooted forward on her chair and held Emilia's expression firmly. "You are brave, my lady."

Emilia shifted and her cheeks darkened to a fetching pink. "Thank you. I don't feel very brave at present."

"That is when moving forward is *most* brave," Richard said with as kind a smile for her as Zara had shared. Only Huxley was silent, simply observing with no discernible emotion about the situation. Richard continued, "We don't know each other well. Even Mr. Wren only knows our family in the barest sense, but you came here. You were vulnerable enough to share this story with us. Will you tell me what you need?"

Emilia glanced up at Wren and then toward Aiden. "I admit, I don't know why Wren brought us here, what he thinks you three might be able...or even willing to do to help me."

"We need to help her exit the country," Aiden said. "Without her husband being able to track where she goes."

"And I know very well that Mr. Huxley and Miss Cooper have some experience in disguise and change of identity," Wren added.

"Ah," Huxley said, pushing from the fireplace where he stood at last. "I see. And where will you take her?"

"My thought was Athawick," Aiden said, and glanced toward Emilia.

Her eyes went wide. "Athawick?" She looked at Wren. "You don't seem surprised by this. You two have already clearly come up with some plan."

"It's far enough away that you would be safe," Aiden said, but Wren could tell his gentle words didn't appease her.

"And it's an open-minded sort of place, I've heard," Zara said. "Where three lovers might live almost entirely openly."

"That's part of the attraction," Wren admitted, and knew Emilia wouldn't like what came next. Or at least she would resist it. "We need three new identities."

"No!" Emilia said as she jumped to her feet. "We've talked about this! I won't destroy you."

"Emilia," Aiden said softly, reaching for her.

She dodged him. "Do you not think I want to be with you two? Do you not know that it breaks me into pieces to think of losing you? But it also crushes me to think you'd turn yourselves inside out to be with me. That you'd let go of your own futures in trade for mine. I won't allow it!" She turned toward Huxley. "You're quiet, but you're clearly the one who understands this situation best."

"And how did you determine that, my lady?" Huxley asked in affected boredom, though his gaze flitted up and down her frame with an increased interest.

"It's obvious if one has eyes in their head," she snapped. "If you'll help me, I would be forever in your debt. But perhaps you can do me another favor and make these two see…see…" She burst into tears suddenly and then raced from the room.

Wren jumped to his feet, moving to follow, but Huxley caught his arm and held him in place. "Let me," he said softly.

Wren tugged his arm away and jerked his face up to the other man's. He still couldn't read him. That was Huxley's gift, it seemed. "You don't know her."

"Oh yes. I do. I know this, at least," he said. "Zara, why don't you and Richard help Mr. Wren and Mr. Edwards? I'll be along shortly."

"Of course," Zara said, and got up. She tucked her arm into Richard's and motioned Aiden and Wren toward the door. "Why don't we go to Richard's study and continue our work there?"

Aiden's lips were a thin line of worry, but he followed the pair from the room regardless. Wren moved to do the same, but at the door he paused and looked back at Huxley. "You'll be gentle with her?"

Huxley's brow wrinkled. "Would you leave me alone with her if you thought I would be harsh?"

"No," Wren said softly. "I suppose I wouldn't. Th-thank you, Huxley, for being willing to help."

He inclined his head and Wren departed to catch up with the others. He could only hope now that whatever this man said to Emilia, it could persuade her to try for a future that he and Aiden couldn't seem to convince her of.

CHAPTER 12

Emilia

Emilia clenched and unclenched her fists against the rough stone of the terrace wall as she looked with unseeing eyes over the well-tended garden below. She could hardly breathe with the weight of uncertainty pressing against her chest. The weight of guilt.

"It's a lovely garden, isn't it?"

She turned to watch Peregrine Huxley exit the house. He walked across the terrace with a surprising grace of movement and stopped beside her. He drew a cigar from the inside pocket of his jacket and lit it with flint, then puffed out a perfect ring of smoke so that it floated away from her.

"I apologize for my outburst," Emilia said softly. "What you must think of me."

"I think you're human and that if you didn't have emotions in this situation, you would likely have something very wrong with you."

She looked at him. He was very handsome and had a bright

intelligence to his eyes—she could see why Zara and Mr. Fitzroy were attracted to him. "Thank you, Mr. Huxley."

"Hux," he said softly. "I don't go by Mister anything." He drew a long breath of his cigar and puffed another ring. "I was once like you, you know."

"Like me?" she said.

"Hard to picture, isn't it? That we could be alike when our positions are so disparate." He chuckled. "But it turns out I have emotions, too."

She faced him. "Of course you do. But I don't think you mean that is how we were alike. So what *do* you mean?"

"I wanted to protect them." He motioned toward the house with his cigar. "I was willing to leave them to do it. To break myself into a thousand pieces just so I wouldn't leave even a hairline crack on them."

She swallowed, for that description did feel too familiar. "Why?"

"Because *I* was the reason your Wren was chasing us. Or I thought I was. I would have sacrificed myself to the man who hired him because I thought that was all I was worth after all I'd done and seen. But they wouldn't let me. Thank God they didn't."

"But your situation is different. Clearly you found a way to continue to protect them."

"Yes. Wren helped us, which is why we owe him." Hux's jaw set a fraction, and in that moment Emilia saw how dangerous the man could be. "I owe him everything."

"My husband won't let go so easily," Emilia said. "He needs me taken care of so he can marry someone else and produce the heirs he hates me for never giving him. He can only do that if my…situation is resolved. He'll do everything in his power to destroy Wren and Aiden. He'll do it for fun, Mr…*Hux*."

"Yes, they are good at that. Men of power. You didn't want to marry him, you said earlier."

"No, I was forced, as is the way of these things so often," she said.

"And your whole life, you were made to turn away from everything you wanted, everything you needed to make some other poxy fuck happy, whether it was a father or an uncle or a husband not worth a third of those two inside."

She pressed her lips together. "Yes."

"And now you'll give away the same happiness, not to mention steal it from them in the process, instead of grabbing it with both hands, drawing a line in the sand and declaring *no more.*"

Her breath caught because those impassioned words hit her in the chest, wrapped around her aching heart and squeezed. "Will they resent me for taking what they've built, though?" she asked, more to herself than to him, though he answered regardless.

"I don't know. I don't see that in either of their eyes when they look at you. But I guarantee they'll resent you for walking away again if you do that."

She stared up into this man's face and saw all the ways their lives had been different and yet all the ways they were the same. She saw her own future, a shining and happy one. And yet she still feared.

"I'll think about what you've said," she murmured.

He nodded. "Do that. May I escort you back inside so you can help with the planning?"

He extended an arm to her and she took it without hesitation. While he guided her back into the house, she asked, "Is it everything you wish it to be…being with them?"

There was a hesitation and she saw a world of emotion flicker over Hux's handsome face. "Oh yes. More than I deserve, perhaps, everything I need and want. I would go to war to keep them with me." They reached the study where she could hear the others talking. Hux looked at her before they entered. "I hope you'll do the same. It's worth it."

He took her into the room before she could respond. And as she crossed to the two men she loved more than anything in the world, she wondered if she was strong enough to fight as Hux had. She feared she'd soon find out.

～

Aiden

"It was kind of them to ask us to stay here tonight," Aiden said as he crossed the large chamber where Richard Fitzroy had put their threesome up for the night.

"It was," Wren agreed, but he was watching Emilia.

Aiden did the same. Since her outburst earlier and then her return to the group with Huxley, she had been pensive and quiet. He and Wren had been giving her space but now, closed up in this lovely room with its big bed and roaring fire...when it was just them, he knew they'd have to discuss the future. He just hoped it wouldn't be for the last time.

"Emilia," he began.

She lifted her gaze from where she'd been staring at the dancing flames in the fire grate and nodded. "I know. I know, Aiden." She stepped forward with a heavy sigh and paced the room restlessly. "What would you each do if we were to go to Athawick together?"

Wren glanced at Aiden and there was such hope on his wonderful face that Aiden could hardly breathe. He widened his eyes, hoping Wren could read his thoughts, would understand that they had to go slow if they were to convince her.

"I have connections with the royal family there," he said carefully. "They are forming a new government and I know for a fact that the king would like help as they navigate those waters."

Her lips parted. "Oh. I didn't know."

Aiden smiled at her. "Because you didn't let me tell you, you were so driven to protect me and Wren from ourselves."

She bent her head. "It's what we've always done, isn't it?"

Wren moved to her and wrapped an arm around her gently. He was also careful now as he said, "We had no one else to protect us, not truly, and so we all fought to become a balm to each other. And it is a wonderful drive...and also a terrible one."

She nodded and Aiden stared as she looked up into Wren's face with such adoration and love. It was powerful and beautiful and he could watch their connection forever. He so desperately wanted to.

"So Aiden will have a future there," she said. "But what about you, Wren?"

"I'm sure I could build new connections there. Transitions of the kind the royal family in Athawick is trying to enact are always fraught with troubles. I'm sure they'd also welcome an experienced investigator to assist with thorny troubles. And if they wouldn't? Then I'll find something else to do. I'll become a fisherman or a shopkeep or…or a vicar."

At that, Emilia laughed. "A bit too wicked for that, aren't you?"

Wren grinned. "Perhaps."

"Emilia, I swear to you," Aiden said, finally stepping closer and joining their circle of devotion and love. He drew his fingers into her hair and placed his opposite hand on Wren's hip. "I swear to you that the future together will be so much better than any future apart."

She seemed to ponder that a moment. "Hux said something to me on the terrace this afternoon. He said that I might not be able to guess that you would resent me for drawing you away from your lives. But I can't forget that there would also be resentment if I took away what we could be to each other."

"I would never resent you, no matter what decisions you made," Aiden said. "But we've lost too much time together due to fear. I don't want to lose another moment."

"Please, Emilia," Wren whispered before he bent his head and kissed her. When she relaxed against him, he drew back and turned her toward Aiden so he could do the same. He tucked her closer to him, loving how her body molded to his so perfectly, reveling in her flavor, the way her tongue swirled with his in a dance of pleasure.

He drew back with difficulty. Now was the time to ask her for what he and Wren wanted. One last time, and pray it would be enough. "Please, please my love. Choose *us.*"

~

Emilia

Emilia was shaking as she stared into the eyes of the two men she loved, standing there together, arms around each other, waiting for her to decide what their futures would hold. Her fears remained, but they had been softened considerably by her conversation earlier in the day with Hux and this one tonight. What had definitely become stronger was her hope.

She had hope for what they could share and be together in the new life they could make in Athawick. She had hope to be happy again, as she hadn't truly been until they had been reunited.

The hope won. She nodded slowly. "Yes," she said, her voice breaking and her eyes stinging with tears of joy. "*Yes*. I want a life together. I always have. And if you two are brave enough to risk it, I must be too."

They moved on her together, Wren's mouth finding hers, Aiden's arms gripping around them both. What started as a happy embrace of love, though, swiftly shifted to something more heated. Wren turned his face toward Aiden and their mouths met, too, as Emilia began to unbutton Wren's jacket. She needed these men, both of these men. She needed to stake the final claim on the future they would build.

She needed pleasure after this day of worry and fear and, at last, surrender.

They were wordless as they touched and kissed and undressed each other. After so many days and nights this way, it was all so *easy*. Aiden unbuttoned her gown as she shoved Wren's jacket away and tugged the buttons of his shirt so he could pull it over his head. Immediately she put her mouth on his skin, sucking a path down his chest while she pushed her dress away. As she dropped to her knees to unfasten his trousers, Wren undressed Aiden and the two men kissed above her.

She pulled Wren's cock to her lips. She stroked the sensitive head against her cheek before she licked him and finally took him into her throat.

He made a garbled sound of pleasure and Aiden's husky laugh made her pussy clench with need. She glanced up at Wren, smiling at him from around his cock. He shook his head.

"You two will be the death of me," he said, but he didn't pull away. Instead he unfastened Aiden's fall front and lowered the placard.

Emilia groaned around his cock and slid him free from her lips, instead stroking him with her hand as she turned her attention to Aiden. She swirled her tongue around his length and sucked him gently. Back and forth she pleasured them with her mouth, loving how they surged for her, needy and panting between their own sweet, passionate kisses.

"Please," she panted at last as she got back to her feet. "I need you both. Now!"

She didn't have to ask twice. They staggered toward the bed together, hands stroking and mouths seeking. Wren leaned against the high edge and caught her by the hips, lifting her up as she let out a squeal of surprise. He positioned her carefully and Aiden reached between them to help Wren take her in one wet stroke. She ground against him, wild with passion. Already her sensitive body trembled, pleasure inching up with every relentless thrust.

Aiden had stepped away, but now she felt him at her back again. He kissed her shoulders, licked her neck as she moaned and then his fingers trailed down her spine and into the globes of her arse.

Wren slowed his thrusts as Aiden prepared her for his cock. She whimpered at how he teased the rosette of her bottom, then stretched her deliciously with his fingers. When she was so close to the edge that she feared she'd fall without him, he pressed his cock to her and glided forward.

She came at once with the fullness of them, the feel of them rubbing together inside of her. She bucked between them as they worked her back and forth, their hands gripping at each other, their mouths sucking her skin.

"Fuck," Wren groaned as he came hot and heavy inside of her.

She whimpered as she kissed him, sucking his tongue gently before she drew back and smiled at him. "Play with him," she whispered. "I want him to lose control."

Wren's eyes lit up and he nodded as he slipped from beneath her, leaving her to bend over the edge of the bed as Aiden continued to slowly fuck her arse. She looked over her shoulder, watching him track Wren as he moved around behind Aiden. She could tell when he'd begun to finger him by the way Aiden's thrusts increased.

She ground back against him, shoving a hand between her own shaking legs, bringing herself back to the edge with only a few strokes of her fingers. She came a second time as Aiden pulled his cock from inside of her and the heat of him splashed over her back and bottom, a tattoo of their pleasure, though only temporarily written on her heated flesh.

As they all collapsed forward, pulling themselves onto the bed weakly, arms and legs entangling, Emilia couldn't help but smile. This was her life now. Her future, as it always should have been.

And there was nothing that could take the joy of it away.

CHAPTER 13

Wren

The dock was loud, a cacophony of sounds and smells and sights between those readying to board the ship to Athawick and the workers loading cargo and luggage. It was a rainbow of the humanity of London and one Wren realized he would likely never see again. It was odd that he felt very little sadness at the thought of never returning to the place he'd called home his entire life.

In truth, Emilia and Aiden were home. Everything else was smoke and mirrors. Existence and nothing more. And now it was over and the future he had hoped for and dreamed of was just a ship's voyage away.

Once Emilia had agreed that they should all leave together, everything had moved at record pace. Richard and Hux had somehow procured passage to Athawick under false names and Zara had done a fine job disguising all of them enough that they wouldn't be instantly recognized by those around them if anyone took particular interest.

Now they awaited their turn to board the ship after warm good-byes to their friends and saviors. Wren wanted to feel excited and free, but until they had sailed away from London, his fear remained heavy in his chest. He kept looking around, watching every face to be certain none were observing their party with more than a passing glance.

At last, a porter reached them and examined their documents and luggage. He stamped a few pages and then gathered up their things. "These will be put in your stateroom, Mr. Vickers," he said to Aiden, using the false name without any hint of suspicion. "You may board the vessel at any time between now and when the first bell rings."

"Thank you," Aiden said, pressing a coin into the man's palm before he turned to smile at Wren and Emilia. "Shall we?"

Emilia nodded, her eyes bright with relief as she turned to look once more at the city behind them. But as she did so, Wren saw the color leave her cheeks and she staggered slightly.

"Well, well, Emilia," came a voice from behind them.

Now Wren spun around and Aiden took a long step forward, hands outstretched for protection as Lord Wilburn, himself, stepped down the dock, his gaze narrowed on Emilia and the two men. Wren tried to put himself in front of her, but he knew it was useless. Despite everything he'd done to put this man off the scent, now he was here.

It was too late to stop whatever would happen next.

Emilia

Emilia had never been one to faint, but the moment she watched Wilburn stalk toward her, his intense stare locked on her face, her vision began darken and her knees trembled. How many times had she watched him do the same over the years, his anger plain on his face? She had known there would be punishment then and she knew the same now.

"W-Wilburn," she whispered, almost without sound.

His lips pinched. "You recall your husband's name, it seems, though not your wifely duties." He glanced now at Aiden and Wren and his disgust rippled over his features. "And here is my whore wife's lover and the very man I hired to find them."

"Watch yourself," Aiden growled, moving toward him before Wren caught his arm and pulled him back. Emilia was glad of both the desire to protect her and the act to protect him.

"What are you doing here?" Emilia asked. She felt foolish to do so, but her mind was spinning. They had been so close to escape. "How did you know *I* was here?"

Wilburn shook his head. "Did you think I had only hired Mr. Wren to find you? No, I have spies everywhere and there were whispers that you were back in London. *And* that you were trying to flee. Why I'm here is to bring you home. You belong to me, Emilia."

"No," Wren said, touching her shoulder and drawing her back toward them. "She doesn't."

Wilburn stared harder and his eyebrows lifted. "And here I thought you and Mr. Edwards were rivals. Perhaps I misunderstood. Spreading your legs for both of them, are you?"

Emilia lifted her chin. "You've had your own dalliances. What do you care?"

"As I said, you belong to me. In the eyes of the law and God, you are my property. And you *will* return home. Now. If you refuse, I can make things much worse than they already are."

He meant for Wren and Aiden, and it was clear by the quiet rage on his face that he would follow through on those threats. The Emilia of weeks before, months before, years before, might have done as he asked to appease him. To give Aiden and Wren a chance to escape. But she wasn't that woman anymore. She was no longer hopeless from losing the loves of her life. She was no longer fearful of an endless future of pain and worry.

"You don't want me, Wilburn," she said softly. "You come to

collect me only to save face. And I know that if I go with you, you'll kill me in the end."

His gaze narrowed and she thought he looked surprised. Apparently he didn't know she had become wise to his plots against her. "And why would you think that?"

"Because I didn't breed you sons to carry on your title. It was all you wanted from me. You won't spend the time and money, nor risk the scandal for a divorce. So you intend to wipe me off the face of the earth and then remarry."

His lips pinched. "You are delusional, Emilia. Hysterical."

She shivered at his use of words that had sent many a good woman to Bedlam for her so-called sins. But it would not be her. "I am getting on the ship with these men," she said, slowly and succinctly. "You will not stop me. You won't interfere."

"And why is that?" Wilburn asked.

She glanced back at Aiden and Wren. They were both tense, coiled and ready to strike. But she wanted to end this a different way. It was so perfectly clear now.

"Because your wife is dead," she said. "She died when I left you. It is not Emilia, Viscountess of Wilburn who will board this vessel and sail from London, never to be seen again. It will be a woman you never met." She stepped toward him even as Aiden grabbed for her hand and tried to keep her close.

Wilburn's gaze flitted over her, though and she could see she had sparked his interest.

"Declare me dead," she said. "I died in an accident, I drowned in the sea and my body never washed up, I wasted away from a venereal disease, I don't care what you say. Take all that I have, all that I brought to our marriage financially. And move on." She tilted her head. "Or challenge me here on this dock, and these two men will still ensure I escape, but I will make every day of your life as much of a living hell as you made mine."

She felt Aiden and Wren move, flanking her on either side, steady and intimidating as they all stared down a man who had ruled over her for the last time. His cheek twitched and then he nodded. "That is acceptable. But if you ever step foot in England again—"

"Careful now," Wren said softly. "I wouldn't finish that sentence."

Wilburn let out his breath in a shaky sigh, and then he pivoted and walked away. She watched him and it was only when he had disappeared out of sight that her knees buckled and Wren and Aiden caught her to hold her up.

"Come, let's board," Aiden said, rushing the two of them up the gangplank and onto the relative safety of the ship.

They were directed to the stateroom they would share, though Emilia hardly heard the words of the servants who directed them, nor saw the lovely room that Richard Fitzroy had somehow procured at the last moment. Her mind spun too much on what she had just done. She had rid herself at last of the man who had ruled and ruined her world for nearly a decade.

And she had killed her old self in the process. Fully stepped into the future. She didn't know whether to laugh or cry.

Aiden shut the stateroom door and then he and Wren were coming to her, their arms sliding around her, their comfort loosening some of her fear.

"You were magnificent," Aiden said against her hair. "My God, it was like watching an empress."

"I only hope it will work," Emilia murmured. "That he will hold to his side of the bargain and not seek me out again."

"When we get to Athawick, we'll change our names to something more permanent," Wren promised as he drew back. "He won't know them. And I doubt he'll waste time on it since I assume he has been heartily compensated for his loss by whatever you just granted him."

"Far too much," Aiden said with a frown. "Your money had been well-invested, Emilia. It is no small sum."

"No sum is too large to be free of him," she said.

Wren paced away and moved to the window of the stateroom

where he looked out on the dock below. The bell had begun to ring and the last passengers were boarding in a rush. "I hate that he'll escape, though. That he won't be punished for his ill deeds and will even be free to commit more against whatever poor woman he marries next."

Emilia smiled slightly and Aiden cocked his head. "What is that look?"

Now she laughed because her freedom was truly beginning to set in and it felt like everything right and wonderful. "He won't, I don't think. This morning as we were saying our goodbyes, Huxley whispered to me not to worry about Wilburn. That his specialty was making sure pricks, as he called them, got what was coming to them. So Wilburn will not be unscathed, I don't think."

Wren's eyes widened. "I pity the man who gets on Hux's bad side."

They stared at each other, smiling as the ship began to move. And then they moved to each other again, their arms around each other, the truth of what was happening so powerful and true that it was almost too much.

"We are free," Emilia whispered. "Free to live. Free to love one another. All of us."

Aiden pulled back and looked at them both and then he whispered, "If it wasn't all of us, it had to be none of us. But by God, I prefer this way."

"As do I," Wren and Emilia murmured.

And then they kissed, just as they had when they'd parted all those years ago. A joining of three mouths, three bodies, three hearts that somehow made up one whole.

And it was everything to Emilia. As it would be for the rest of her life.

EPILOGUE

One Year Later
Wren

Wren was no longer Wren, not really. He went by Mr. Fowler and had for many months. It was still something he laughed about with Emilia and Aiden, the idea of changing his name to something that contained the word *fowl*. They still called him Wren in the safety of their beautiful, bright green home by the sea. Just as when they were alone he continued called them by the names they'd always gone by, rather than the new identities the former royal family of Athawick had helped them create.

They had all taken to Athawick as soon as they arrived. Aiden had been correct that King Grantham—who now went as Mr. Alexander, turning one of his many middle names into his last when he became prime minister—did wish for his assistance. Aiden had quickly risen in the ranks of the new government and it was evident he adored his work.

Wren had *not* become a fisherman, as he had claimed he would be happy to do. He had instead taken a position under the prime minister's mother, Queen Mother Giabella, in her charitable society. Even Emilia had taken a place as the former king's wife's personal secretary. She served Ophelia Alexander as a friend, confidante and valued organizer and assistant.

And now as Wren walked up the sandy, twisting lane to that home he so loved, he could hear Aiden and Emilia already inside, their voices drifting from the open window. They were laughing as they talked about their respective days.

He knew they would be even more joyous when he shared the letter he had received directly from the messenger off the boat earlier in the day. The one from Peregrine Huxley that told of the untimely and rather painful death of the Viscount of Wilburn at the hand of the brother of a lady he had been trying to court. Her refusal had led to a violent scene and eventual dual between the two men.

Huxley's smug tone in the missive made Wren think he might have had more of a hand in the outcome than Wren could imagine, but either way he was pleased. Emilia was truly free.

His heart swelled with it. A year ago none of them could have known how happy they could be. How loved they could be. How perfect their life could look and feel.

He opened the door and stepped inside of that life once more, and his smile widened as the two loves of his life rushed to him, talking over each other, kissing him and each other. The heavenly scents of food drifted from the dining room down the hallway.

He was home. And there was no greater pleasure than the knowledge that he would never have to leave the home that was them again.

ALSO BY JESS MICHAELS

Theirs

Their Marchioness

Their Duchess

Their Countess

Their Bride

Their Viscountess

The Kent's Row Duchesses

No Dukes Allowed

Not Another Duke

Not the Duke You Marry

Regency Royals

To Protect a Princess

Earl's Choice

Princes are Wild

To Kiss a King

The Queen's Man

The Three Mrs

The Unexpected Wife

The Defiant Wife

The Duke's Wife

The 1797 Club

The Daring Duke

Her Favorite Duke

The Broken Duke

The Silent Duke

The Duke of Nothing

The Undercover Duke

The Duke of Hearts

The Duke Who Lied

The Duke of Desire

The Last Duke

To see a complete listing of Jess Michaels' titles, please visit:

http://www.authorjessmichaels.com/books

www.ingramcontent.com/pod-product-compliance
Lightning Source LLC
Chambersburg PA
CBHW021720190726

48289CB00008B/2617